W9-AMQ-070

THE UNEXPECTED HERO

By
Michael C. Grumley

1.2

AUTHOR'S NOTE

Like the first book, this is an episodic; a more complex story line written in shorter, faster installments. And while this book can also be enjoyed as a standalone, reading the first will deepen the story.

Finally, any similarities to real events and experiences...are not entirely coincidental.

Michael

OTHER BOOKS BY
MICHAEL GRUMLEY

BREAKTHROUGH

LEAP

AMID THE SHADOWS

THROUGH THE FOG

THE UNEXPECTED HERO

FOREWORD

She couldn't believe it.

Dr. Shannon Mayer sat next to her daughter, staring down at her beautiful brown hair, still unable to believe it all. It was a miracle in every sense of the word.

Ellie was leaning forward, drawing on a large piece of paper atop her mother's desk. She didn't know what "play therapy" was, nor could she understand that it was just the beginning of a very long recovery. To her, she was simply home.

Shannon studied Ellie's picture. Drawing was a common technique for helping victims externalize traumatic memories and to bring them out where they could be dealt with. But it would take time. A long time. So far it had only been a week, and Shannon was still reeling from the shock of finding Ellie alive.

She had been missing for over eighteen months, kidnapped and held by a lunatic with a deeply disturbed view of the world. Someone who wanted something much more from Shannon Mayer than just her daughter. He wanted Shannon herself.

To make matters worse, Shannon and her husband had long since reached the end of their ropes. Suffering from exhaustion and depression, both were drowning in their own despair when the miracle they so desperately needed walked into their lives.

She heard a knock on the door and gently placed her hand on Ellie's back as she stood up. She crossed the eerily silent room, with her steps making only the slightest sound against the thick, ornate carpet. When she reached the door, she glanced back at Ellie, still coloring away. Shannon's emotions were like a series of ocean waves, washing over her again and again. Disbelief that Ellie was actually home, followed by a sudden and overwhelming sense of elation. Then came the dread of knowing what truly lay in front of Ellie: a lifelong effort to repair the damage, emotionally and mentally.

Shannon took a deep breath and reached for the door, pulling it open.

"Hello, Evan."

"Hi," he said, stepping into the room. He spotted Ellie at the large desk with the paper in front of her.

"Ellie, honey, look who's here. It's Evan."

Ellie wore a beautiful white dress with blue and green flowers, and her hair was pulled back into a ponytail. She stopped drawing and looked up at Evan. With a smile, she quickly jumped up, trotted around the desk, and wrapped her little arms around his waist.

Evan responded by bending over and shyly wrapping his own arms around her. "Hi, Ellie. How are you?"

"Good."

Dr. Mayer held her hand softly over her mouth as she watched the tender moment. Evan Nash was her miracle. Not just for Shannon but for her entire family. If it weren't for him, Ellie never would have been found in time. If not for his accident.

It all began with a serious accident, seemingly common by any other standard until the young high school student began experiencing strange visions.

Visions which Shannon Mayer suspected were illusions caused by a concussion during the accident. She continued having doubts even when Evan reported "seeing" strange images. It wasn't until she tested him for herself that that she became a believer. For his sake and for hers.

Shannon eventually realized that Evan wasn't experiencing illusions or hallucinations. Instead, he was seeing something very real. But there was something more frightening below the surface. His body was experiencing very dangerous reactions during the episodes, reactions that even now, were still trying to kill him. And as the visions increased, so did the harrowing toll it took on his body until he eventually ended up in a coma.

And yet, through it all, after recovering and even in the face of danger, Evan sacrificed it all, using his "curse" to find Shannon's missing daughter. And find her he did.

But Evan was still in danger. The visions had not dissipated even with medication. Nor did his symptoms weaken. The drug was only masking the problem until help arrived. Help in the form of Shannon Mayer's sister, Mary.

While Evan was in the hospital, Mary and a friend had discovered something startling. A piece of information, which gave them hope that Evan might survive after all. But that hope was resting on little more than an old medical journal and two nurses hell-bent on locating one individual reportedly to have had the same symptoms as Evan's; twenty years before.

That person had made every effort to disappear and even managed to have himself declared dead. What he wasn't expecting though, were the brains and tenacity of both Mary and her friend. Not only did they eventually find him...but Mary was bringing him back with her, *today*.

Shannon finally blinked the tears away and lowered her hand onto Evan's shoulder as he straightened. "Come, have a seat."

He nodded from beneath a head of straight, light-brown hair and moved away from the door, stopping next to the familiar leather chair.

After watching Ellie return to the desk to resume her artwork, Shannon turned to the teenager. "How are things?"

"Pretty good. My mom got a new job."

"Is that right?"

"Yeah. A customer in her restaurant told her he'd been watching her and that he wanted to hire her to manage the wait staff at his own restaurant. Some fancy place in Montrose. So we're going to look at a new apartment tonight."

Shannon smiled warmly. "That's great."

"And get this, the man — his name is Mr. Friedricks — also said he has an old car he's selling and asked if I wanted to buy it. He said I could work part-time at his restaurant to pay it off."

"Incredible." She was happy to see Evan excited, even for the moment. He had done so much for her. Things she would never truly be able to pay back. But it didn't mean she couldn't try. It would be a breach of ethics to compensate him directly. However, Glendale was a fairly well-to-do city just outside of Los Angeles, and over the years Shannon had garnered a lot of favors through her practice. She couldn't pay Evan anything but that didn't prevent her from making a few phone calls.

"And how are you feeling?" she asked, changing the subject.

"Better. Still healing though."

"That's not what I meant."

"Oh." He glanced over again at Ellie, her head down and a colored marker working away in her hand. "The Valium helps, but it feels like it's wearing off. The pain is coming back."

It was the pain that had nearly killed Evan. Or more specifically, the internal trauma that was causing it. It traced back to his accident and was the reason he had come to her in the first place. A meeting she never dreamed would result in Evan risking his life to save her own daughter.

Shannon's expression grew serious. "Evan, I think we need to stop with the Valium."

"Why?"

Because she had received a call from her sister that morning, she thought. *A call that told Shannon she needed to see Evan as quickly as possible, and put an end to the medication.*

Shannon glanced at her watch as another knock sounded from the other side of the door.

"Come in."

Her receptionist Tania pushed open the door and looked at them both. "She's here."

Shannon glanced at the confused look spreading across Evan's face. She then headed toward the door, arriving just as her sister, Mary Creece, entered behind Tania.

Her sister looked tired, but her eyes intently swept the room, looking for Ellie. When she spotted her niece at Shannon's desk, Mary immediately frowned and began crying, holding her arms out. She dropped to her knees as Ellie jumped from her chair and ran to her, throwing herself into her aunt's arms.

"Thank God," Mary cried, stroking Ellie's soft hair. "Thank God, you're alright."

A tall, older man stepped into the room behind Mary. His hair was thick and gray, and he was dressed in a worn flannel shirt and jeans.

Mary cleared her throat and looked up, still holding Ellie. "Sis, allow me to introduce Daniel Taylor."

Shannon knew exactly who the man was, although he looked very different than she was expecting. Especially considering the incredible trip her sister had undertaken to find him — a man who had gone to great lengths not to be found.

But Daniel Taylor was the only one. He was the only person who understood what was happening to Evan. He understood because he had the same unimaginable affliction.

"It's nice to meet you, Mr. Taylor. I hear you were a hard man to find."

Taylor shook Shannon's hand. "Not hard enough for your sister, apparently."

The large man smiled down at Ellie from under his thick brow. Next he turned and looked at Evan with his piercing brown eyes. "So this is him," Taylor mused. "You're the one who can see things, are you?"

Evan didn't respond. Instead, he took a nervous step backward and glanced at Dr. Mayer.

Taylor followed him, stepping closer. He towered over the teenager and looked him up and down, assessing.

Evan tried to retreat further but ran into the arm of the chair.

A devilish grin slowly spread across Taylor's face. "Relax, boy. I'm not here to hurt you. I'm here to keep it from killing you..."

Taylor turned around and looked at Shannon. He motioned toward her daughter, Ellie, and Mayer took the hint.

"Tania, can you take Ellie next door? She can draw in there."

"Of course." Tania bent down and smiled at the small girl. "Let's get your things."

"Okay."

Everyone waited as the two crossed the room and gathered Ellie's things. Walking back toward the door, Shannon knelt down and gave her daughter a warm squeeze and kiss.

Once gone, Taylor turned back to Evan. "You don't have much time."

He looked nervously to Dr. Mayer. Rounding the chair, he took another step backward.

Taylor gazed down at him intently. "You know it's true, don't you?"

Evan still didn't answer.

"The pain should be in your chest by now. Soon your respiratory system will freeze up, and you won't come back out." He took another step closer. "Trust me. I know what's happening to you. The symptoms may be even stronger in you, which means it's escalating more quickly. In a week, you'll be dead."

"I...I...don't believe you."

A wry grin spread across Taylor's lips and he leaned closer. "Oh, yes, you do. You believe me and you're scared to death."

He was right. Evan had just met the man...but he did believe him. The episodes were rapidly becoming worse again, just like before. And last time he'd ended up in the hospital and barely made it back out alive.

"Evan?"

He looked back at Dr. Mayer, who quietly approached from behind Taylor. Unlike Taylor, her expression was calm and reassuring. Evan promptly stopped his retreat when his right calf bumped against the psychiatrist's leather couch.

"Evan," she said again. "The Valium was a mistake. I'm sorry. I didn't know until Mary called me this morning."

"It makes it worse," Taylor added. "But you know that now, don't you?"

Evan stared at them both before reluctantly nodding.

"And you know what I'm telling you is the truth."

He knew. That morning he was barely able to get out of bed. It felt like his heart simply wanted to stop beating; something he'd never felt before. And it scared the hell out of him. Until recently, most of the stress his body experienced during an episode, he couldn't even feel. Not until he came out of it. But now he could feel it even when he was unconscious, *while* he was having the vision. And now it was happening every night, without fail. After what had happened that morning, Evan was petrified to go to sleep again.

After a long moment, he peered back up at Taylor. "Can you help me?"

Taylor straightened and looked back at both

Shannon and her sister, Mary. "Well, I sure as hell didn't spend three days on a bus for nothing." He motioned behind him. "And next to a woman who wouldn't stop talking."

Evan's composure softened and he reached to the side, leaning slightly on the arm of the couch. Dr. Mayer had told Evan they'd found someone with the same disorder. He didn't know what he had been expecting, but it sure wasn't this.

"So," he said, with a slight shrug. "When do we start?"

"You're out of time, kid. We start right now."

Evan felt a streak of nervousness run down his spine as he thought about something Taylor had just said. Any day could be the day that he didn't wake up again.

What if that day was *today*?

The airport, or LAX, was located sixteen miles from downtown Los Angeles. It was the sixth busiest airport in the world as measured by passenger traffic, serving over sixty-three million passengers a year. Yet it was LAX's fifteen thousand open parking spaces that also made it an ideal destination for finding a throwaway car, complete with a fresh set of plates.

Most cars parked in a lot near a major airport weren't expected to be used for at least a few days, providing him more than enough time to use the white minivan before disposing of it. This one even had plenty of gas.

A hundred and fifty miles later, he reached his search area and began circling. The farther away from where the car would be reported missing, the better.

He'd always mused over how much of the public's knowledge of child abductions was wrong. The vast majority were not committed by strangers, but by family members or acquaintances. Only a fraction were strangers, which in the end, made it that much easier for him. It meant the initial investigation would concentrate primarily on those with some form of connection to the child and, therefore, take several more days before anyone considered someone like him.

He scanned the streets noting the perfectly maintained hedges and trees. The neighborhood was, of course, another help. The more affluent, the more denial everybody was in. Feeling secure behind their metal gates and gleaming security patrol cars, the well-to-do never suspected that they were in fact the ideal targets.

Their affluent children were wrapped in the bubble of false security even more tightly than their parents. They asked for everything, did nothing, and expected it as some kind of birthright. It made them weak. Mentally fragile. And all the reminders in the world wouldn't prevent them from getting into a strange car, given the right amount of incentive and fear. A simple question, getting them close enough to the car to see a gun pointed at them, was all it usually took.

He finally spotted a girl walking by herself on the sidewalk and checked his rearview mirror. The street was almost empty. He pulled over a couple of houses ahead of her and simultaneously slid his hand under a dark piece of cloth on the passenger seat. She looked perfect.

It was easy when you knew what you were doing. This time, the whole thing took less than twenty-five seconds.

Evan sat on the dark leather couch facing Taylor. He turned to watch Dr. Mayer close the window blinds then looked down when Mary, a nurse, gently slid his right index finger into a small pulse oximetry sensor. They had used it before to measure his heart rate and oxygen levels.

Mary noticed Taylor watching her with interest. While she wrapped a small piece of tape around the plastic sensor, she answered the man's question before he could ask it.

"Yes, it's a little crude, but it gives us some warning."

"And then what?"

Mary frowned and looked at Taylor. "Then we scream and shake him until he wakes up." She didn't mention the last time, having to actually slap Evan to pull him out of it.

Taylor looked grimly at Evan. "That's not going to work anymore. He's too far along. The only person who can bring him out now is himself."

Mary paused and exchanged a worried look with her sister Shannon.

Taylor continued watching Evan. He finally glanced at his watch. "Alright, kid, tell me what you see during these 'episodes' of yours."

The experiences had started after a serious bicycle accident, which occurred just weeks before and included a concussion. Thankfully, it was not fatal, but the resulting visions were causing frightening physiological effects. In fact, *effects* were an understatement. The truth was that each episode was slowly sucking the life from him.

"I'm not really sure. It starts off dark and gets lighter until I'm surrounded by it. It looks a lot like...fog. That's the closest thing I can think of."

They all turned as the office door quickly opened. Evan's mother stepped into the room, looking for and finding her son. "Evan, are you all right?"

"Yeah, Mom. I'm fine."

Connie Nash glanced at Shannon, standing a few steps away. Her look was one of gratitude. Shannon had called Evan's mother and stalled until she could get there. It was part of Shannon's promise to the woman that there would be no more attempts with Evan without her knowing about it. And it was not a promise she would soon break considering their tumultuous beginning.

Connie crossed the room and sat down next to Evan on the couch. She took his hand and squeezed it, glancing at Taylor in front of them.

"You must be Mr. Taylor."

Taylor nodded. "Dan."

"Thank you for coming, Dan," she said, wrapping an arm around her son. "Can you help Evan?"

"We were just getting to that. Your son is living on borrowed time, so whatever we're going to do, we'd better hurry."

She turned to Evan with raised eyebrows.

"He's right, Mom. It's getting really bad."

Taylor turned his attention back to Evan. "So, it looks like fog?"

"Yeah, sort of."

"Is it moving?"

"Yes."

"What else?"

"When the fog moves, it kind of opens up. Almost like a tunnel."

"And what do you see in the tunnel?"

Evan shrugged. "I don't know. Different things. People. Places. Sometimes I don't see anything. But the last several nights, I saw stuff, even with the Valium."

"And your reactions?"

Mary spoke up next to him, her eyes still on Evan. "Sweating, heart palpitations, rapid temperature changes in the skin. Combinations that don't make any sense. His heart rate and blood pressure go in opposite directions."

Taylor leaned forward and took a closer look into Evan's eyes. "How are you feeling now?"

"My chest hurts."

After a long moment, Tayler seemed satisfied and leaned back in his chair. "What color?"

"Color?"

"The fog. What color is the fog?"

"Uh...white."

"Do you see any other colors?"

The three women in the room remained quiet. Shannon wondered where Taylor was going with his questioning but said nothing.

"Evan thought about his answer for a moment. Yes. There's red too."

"Where? In the fog or around it?"

"It's more like behind. As the fog moves, I can see patches of red behind it, trying to get through." Evan hesitated. This was the part he had not yet told anyone. "That's when it starts. That's when I start to feel things."

Mary raised her eyebrows, surprised. "You mean that's when the symptoms begin?"

He nodded.

"Wait a minute," Shannon said. "This happens when you see what exactly? The fog?"

"No, when I begin to see what's behind it."

"You mean the red area?" Shannon asked, looking between the two. "Why? What is it?"

Taylor remained quiet, waiting for Evan to answer. But he didn't so Taylor spoke up. "It's not just a color. Is it, Evan?"

Evan shook his head quietly.

"What does that mean? Is it some kind of object?"

"You could say that. I think the kid knows what it is. He certainly should by now. It's not the fog that's causing his body to panic. It's what's behind it. And it's not an object. It's more like…an ocean."

They could see the look of fear growing on Evan's face as Taylor spoke.

"An ocean of what?"

"An ocean of blood…of pain…agony. Whatever you want to call it. That's what's been causing his body to panic. I'm guessing he's been too afraid to tell you, any of you, that what he really sees behind that fog is an endless sea of death."

They were dumbfounded. "What…what does that mean?"

"It doesn't mean anything. It's what it *is*. The kid hasn't told you about this, because I think he already knows what it is. The images he sees are coming from the space that lies between the world of the living and the world of the dead."

4

Connie Nash squeezed her son hard and looked into his eyes. She could see his nervousness. She continued holding his hand as he lay down onto the couch.

The truth was that Evan was terrified. The fear he felt that morning had returned, and he worried what the next "episode" might bring. Now that Dan Taylor had confirmed what was behind the white fog, he felt even worse. And if the affliction really was stronger in Evan, then no one had a clue about what might happen next.

He closed his eyes for a moment, trying to muster enough courage. He tried to appear strong for his mother and hoped she would not sense how much anguish he was really in. *God, why did this have to happen to him? Hadn't his life been hard enough?*

Evan opened his eyelids, revealing tears glistening beneath them. He blinked hard and rolled to the left, looking at Taylor.

"What do I do?"

Taylor took a deep breath. "Listen to me very carefully. Your body is panicking because it *knows* what's behind that fog. It knows what death feels like, and it knows how close it is. You can't let your body forget where it really is: here and alive."

"How do I do that?"

Taylor quietly undid the top button on his shirt. He then reached beneath the neckline and pulled something out.

Evan could see it was a long string of some kind. No, not a string…a chain. He watched Taylor pull it all the way out, before lifting it up and over his head.

"Take this," he said, holding it out. Most of the silver chain was bunched in his hand with a pendant hanging over the tips of his fingers.

"What is it?"

He motioned for Evan to put it on. "It's your way home."

Evan complied, sliding it down over his ruffled hair. He turned the pendant over in his hand and studied it. The dark, polished metal was formed in the shape of a cross.

Taylor leaned forward and wrapped his giant hand over Evan's. "Keep it in your hand."

He nodded.

"Keep your hand tight. You need to keep squeezing it hard enough to be able to feel that cross while you're on the other side."

"Huh?"

"But not too hard that you can't fall asleep."

Evan stared at him a moment, and then squeezed tightly until the cross caused a tinge of pain in his palm.

This time he was less worried about falling asleep. He could feel the pills Taylor gave him begin to kick in. Some kind of extract. Evan felt his mind begin to slip and pressed harder until feeling the pain in his hand again. He tried to remember the names of the extracts; hops and something called chamomile.

His mind slipped again. It was working fast.

"Now listen closely," Taylor said, in a low voice. "The ocean that lies behind the fog is death. Don't forget that, ever. The closer it gets to you, the more your body will panic until it simply can't take it anymore. And that's when your life is over." He placed a hand over Evan's and squeezed, pressing Evan's palm tighter around the pendant. "Remember where you really are. Focus on this and nothing else."

Evan nodded, fighting back tears then looked up at his mother.

She was still gripping his other hand firmly in both of hers, pulling it close to her. Her voice was trembling. "I'm not leaving you, Evan. I'm right here."

"I'm scared again."

"Good," Taylor replied. "Fear will help you. Don't let go, no matter how close it gets to you. When you feel that fear take hold, remember what you have in your hand and repeat this: 'Though I walk through the valley of the shadow of death, I will fear no evil.'"

Evan looked at him with surprise. "What?"

"Repeat it."

After a long pause, Evan repeated the phrase.

"Again."

Evan blinked and complied. He was losing his fight against Taylor's extract pills.

"Good. Use the pendant and repeat that over and over. Don't stop saying it and, whatever you do, stand your ground."

Evan stammered. "But I'm not religious."

Taylor furrowed his brow at the boy. "Neither am I."

It seemed like only moments after everyone around him had disappeared before he saw something. The fog began small but grew larger and larger until it filled his view, moving and swirling around him.

It felt cool as it moved past.

He could sense it moving through his fingers and hair. Like a cool but eerie breeze. There came a strange feeling as the fog thickened around him.

Evan looked back where the fog had come from and could see a small, seemingly tight, circle forming. As it expanded, it resembled a horizontal tornado, slowly spinning and opening wider, allowing him to peer further down its center. He watched it widen further and further.

Then he felt it.

It began subtly. A faint tingle in his chest. The grip of panic.

Ahead of him, the tunnel grew larger. But this time there were no images inside. Instead, the other side began to thin and change color. The white swirl gradually began to turn pink.

Now a jolt of panic ran through Evan, causing him to lurch. His body knew what was coming through the tunnel as if pulled by a powerful magnet. The pink color of fog grew darker and continued swirling. It was impossible to tell if it was getting closer or the tunnel was simply growing larger.

The color deepened noticeably again and another jolt coursed through his body. This time it wasn't just panic. He had never felt pain on the other side before, until now. And the fear was stronger than ever.

The inside of the tunnel began to grow red, and a powerful feeling of dread washed over him. He could feel his breathing, or what he thought was his breathing, becoming erratic.

Evan saw several other red circles begin appearing through the fog. He forced himself to remember what Taylor had said. He was in a place between life and death and had to stand his *ground. He couldn't lose the connection to the living, no matter what.*

He concentrated and tried to squeeze his right hand, but felt nothing. He tried again and again until he finally had something. A tiny point of pressure. Evan concentrated harder. He soon felt multiple points against his palm. It was the cross. Taylor's cross.

In front of him, dozens of red dots quickly became hundreds. Through some of the larger patches, he could now see actual blood. His body was hyperventilating now and beginning to shake. He concentrated desperately on his hand. The pendant was still there.

Blood became visible everywhere. Evan squeezed his hand harder and spoke to himself.

"Though I walk through the valley of the shadow of death, I will fear no evil…"

5

The northwest corner of East Broadway and Glendale Boulevard held an old and very dark secret of which most city residents remained unaware. During its very first years in the early twentieth century, a three-story Victorian structure with seventy-five spacious rooms occupied the site and was known by another, more somber name: the Glendale Sanitarium. Now, over a century later, the very same ground was home to a more modern and well-known enterprise called the Glendale Beeline Transit System.

The connection was more than just a little ironic, given the mental state of one of the company's bus drivers. A driver whose route passed the auspicious corner multiple times a day. But today something was different.

Outside the Beeline's giant beige building, along East Broadway, three marked police cars were parked in a straight line just beyond Glendale's busiest downtown stop.

From the opposite direction, waiting for the light to turn green, the bus driver's hands gripped the steering wheel like a vise. He could see the squad cars waiting at his next stop, with two officers standing near the first car. A third officer was in the shade closer to the building, speaking with a man in a dark suit and tie.

Someone honked behind him and the driver

realized his light had already turned green. His mind began to race as he reluctantly pulled forward. As he rounded onto East Broadway, he watched in slow motion as the first two officers turned, hearing the rumbling of his approaching bus. For a brief moment, he contemplated smashing the pedal down and attempting an escape, but he stopped himself. *No one could escape in a bus.* Instead, he fought to keep his cool long enough to pull the giant vehicle to the curb where it jerked to a stop.

His heart beating rapidly, the driver opened the door and simultaneously leaned forward reaching down along the left-hand side of his seat. His fingers instinctively found the small bag he kept with him at all times. He fumbled to get it open while trying to maintain sight of the officers between the shifting forms of his few disembarking passengers.

He could feel his entire body begin shaking as he watched the last passenger step down through the double doors and into the sunlight. His hand was now inside the bag, gripping, ready for the moment he had prepared for. And it was going to happen right here...on his bus.

The seconds ticked by, with each heartbeat pounding heavily in his chest. He twitched his left hand to ensure he could still feel the cool metal against his palm.

But to his shock, none of the officers made a move toward him or his bus, nor was the man in the suit anyone he recognized from administration. Instead, all four men paid him and his bus only a faint acknowledgement before turning back around.

A growing sense of confusion washed over him in a wave. Then he realized. It wasn't him. It was something else.   They were there for something else...or *someone* else.

He promptly pulled his hand out and placed it back onto the wheel before closing the doors.   He nearly stomped on the gas in elation but caught himself and eased his foot gradually onto the accelerator.

No attention.

The powerful bus engine roared beneath him, and he watched intently through the giant side mirrors as the police and their cars faded in the distance.

An uncontrollable grin spread across his face. They didn't know.   They still didn't know...which meant he was doing everything right.

Maybe he *couldn't* be caught.

6

Taylor eased the door closed and turned around to follow Shannon and Mary out into the hallway. "Well, he's still alive."

Taylor explained the nature of the episodes, as Evan called them, to the women. They happened as the mind passed from consciousness to unconsciousness. Not alert enough to be awake but not tired enough to be asleep. And it would only happen once per sleep cycle. After that, the body was far too exhausted for it to occur a second time.

"He made it," whispered Shannon.

"Don't get too excited, Counselor. This is only the beginning. It will get far worse before it gets better, and he'll have to grow stronger to match it."

"What does that mean, 'only the beginning'?"

"It's hard to say."

"How long did it take *you* to make it through this?"

"It's not a matter of making it through," Taylor said. "This will never go away. It will never be gone. I can't tell him how to cure it. I can only teach him how to fight it. How to endure it."

He watched the two women exchange looks. "It took me a few weeks to finally withstand the visions. But I was older. And the curse runs far deeper in this kid than me."

Shannon raised her eyebrows. "Curse?"

"What would you call it?" He lowered his voice. "It's a lot stronger in him. Hell, I don't even know if

I would have made it this far. I'm not going to bullshit you. I don't know if he's going to survive this."

"He has to," Mary whispered.

"Yeah, well, there's a lot more involved here than grit. It's hard to fully explain what he sees on the other side. It's like...standing face to face with the Grim Reaper himself."

"Evan's strong," Shannon insisted. "He can do this."

"Every night?"

"If he has to."

"Your confidence in him is admirable, but naïve," Taylor said. "Fighting every day for a few weeks is one thing, fighting every day for years is another."

"We're not going to give up."

"You've got the easy part," he scoffed. "But it's your prerogative." Taylor looked past them again, toward the end of the hall and the reception area. "I've gotta take a break. Where's the john?"

"Uh, outside. To the left."

Both women watched Taylor advance down the hallway and disappear around the corner.

Shannon turned back to Mary. "How in the world did you ever get him to come here?"

Mary smiled devilishly. "I blackmailed him."

"Really?"

"He's quite paranoid."

"Is that why you took the bus?"

"It was either that or the train. Low security and both accepted all cash payments. He wouldn't let me use my phone either. Otherwise, I would have warned you sooner about the Valium."

"I can't even begin to thank you."

She shrugged. "What are sisters for?"

The truth was that Mary never knew there was a connection between Evan and Ellie. She knew her older sister was hoping for a miracle, but when she left, Mary's priority was simply to save Evan. His health was deteriorating rapidly, and being a nurse, she was not about to give up. With the help of a friend, she set out to find someone who never wanted to be found. Someone who had gone to great lengths to cover his tracks.

It was the phone call that morning that completely shocked Shannon. After Taylor finally relented, Mary called her sister from the bus the second her phone had a signal again. She could not believe it when Shannon practically screamed the incredible news into the phone. Evan had helped Shannon find her missing daughter before she lost her forever.

He was an incredible kid. At eighteen and just a few inches over five feet, he had a streak of raw courage that neither had seen before, even in men twice his size.

Evan opened his eyes and blinked several times. The room looked darker than before, leaving him wondering how long he'd slept. He focused on the bookshelf against the wall and then scanned the room.

There was a soreness in his hand, and he opened it to find the pendant still inside. The indentations were gone, but the pain was still there.

Evan let the cross dangle around his neck and rose up into a sitting position, dropping his feet off the edge of the couch. He worked backward through his memory and was suddenly overcome by a wave of relief. He had done it. He had fought back and he was still here.

He began to grin when the door opened. He turned in time to catch a glimpse of Ellie before she promptly disappeared again, running back down the hall. Evan could hear her yelling excitedly that he was awake.

A minute later the door was pushed open wide and five others walked in behind Ellie. His mother Connie was first, followed by Shannon, Mary, Tania, and finally Dan Taylor.

"You're awake!" Before he could get up, Connie rushed to her son on the couch.

"How do you feel?"

"Better." He couldn't stop himself from grinning. "I think we did it." Everyone smiled at him except Taylor. Evan leaned forward as if he were about to stand up but suddenly stopped. The pain in his chest was still there.

He winced and rolled back onto the couch, clutching his chest. He looked up confused. "It still hurts."

Taylor mused. "I bet it does."

"But, I thought…"

"You thought what? One time would fix it and everything would be fine?" He shook his head. "Boy, you have one hell of a road ahead of you."

The expression on Evan's face changed to shock. "How…how long?"

"I don't know." Taylor didn't know how long. It was either forever, or if he died, much sooner.

Evan dropped his head and stared absently at the

carpeting under his feet. *God, I don't think I can do this.*

"Evan?"

He raised his head back up to see Shannon step forward.

"This is not going to be easy. I understand that. We all do. But we're here to help you." When he didn't answer, she continued. "We're all ready to help you fight this, including Mr. Taylor, if you let us."

"What does that mean?"

Shannon glanced around at the others before turning back to him. "I want you to come stay with me for a while. At my house, with Mr. Taylor. The next few weeks are going to be rough, and he's agreed to stay and help you through it. If he can."

Evan looked at each one of them in the room, beginning with his mother, who was clearly struggling to keep a stiff upper lip. When he got to Taylor again, he asked, "How bad is this going to get?"

"Pretty damn bad."

"Will I make it?"

Taylor did not answer. Instead, he merely stared down with a look that Evan could not read. It looked like either doubt or indifference.

"Mom?"

Connie Nash frowned at her son, her eyes welling up. "I think we need to do this, honey."

Evan lowered his head before finally nodding.

7

"I still feel it. All of it. The pain, the desperation. Even though we have her back, the anguish is still there. Hell, it hasn't even been a week, but I thought those feelings would be mostly gone. Instead it's almost like it's still happening."

Dennis Mayer looked at his daughter, curled up asleep at the table in his wife's lap. "Ellie was the one who was taken, and yet she's recovering faster than we are. We've got a long way to go, but now I realize it's not just about the pain that you let go of; sometimes there's a pain that won't let go of *you*.

"And I can't stop thinking that if I hadn't decided to pick that phone back up and check the messages, I wouldn't be here, with them." Leaning forward slightly with his arms on the table, Dennis looked softly at Shannon. "I'm a changed man. No one can come that close to losing everything and not have it change them. If it doesn't change you, then as far as I'm concerned, you're dead already."

He straightened in his chair. "So I quit the force. I went in and gave them my notice. I'll get a small, partial pension and a healthcare plan. But now, I'll be able to focus on the only thing that matters: my family."

Taylor dropped his head slightly and stared at his coffee cup, gently fingering the edge of the saucer beneath it. It was late, almost midnight, and they were the only three still up. Evan had fallen asleep, thankfully without another episode. Taylor was not expecting another until the next evening. Evan's mother was asleep on the couch in the other room.

Taylor pursed his lips and watched as Shannon softly kissed the top of Ellie's head, careful not to disturb her. "So, she's going to be alright?"

"Only time will tell. But we'll take whatever we can get."

Taylor nodded. He remained quiet for a long time, contemplating. "I've got to tell you, your sister is damn tenacious."

Shannon grinned. "Yes she is."

"No one had found me since Rief died. I thought I'd gotten all the loose ends. I couldn't believe it when her and her friend showed up at the cabin. When it was clear I'd been found out, I wasn't sure what to do." He shook his head slowly. "I'd been hiding for a long time."

Taylor was quiet again, still tapping the saucer in front of him. The memories were as vivid as ever. "Sometimes it's still hard to believe what they were going to do. After all, the government is supposed help you, right? Not kill you. But there's an awful lot of bad things happening in the government these days. The bigger it gets, the more secrets it keeps."

Shannon spoke over the top of Ellie in a hushed tone. "Are you sure they're still after you?"

"No." Taylor shrugged. "But I can't take the chance. I was lucky to escape the first time. And things were different then. It was a small group they'd put together, and they didn't really know what they were doing yet. If it were a couple years later, who knows?"

"What exactly did they want with you?" Dennis

asked.

"They wanted to use me as a weapon. It started off as a defense related project, but I could see their minds turning."

"Who is 'they'?"

"The CIA. I guess one of their higher-ups witnessed a paranormal event, and it drove him to create a special task force to investigate whether it was real. They named it *Project Stargate* and had about ten agents assigned to it. It was run by a specialist named Douglas Bollinger who'd already been a spook for years. One thing I'll give 'em is that they sure picked the right bastard for the job.

"They spent a lot of time tracking down supposed psychics all across the country. Anyone claiming to have abilities. Any kind of ability at all. At first they ran their tests claiming to be a branch under the department of sciences or some bullshit."

"They were looking for people with abilities so they could exploit them?"

"That's right. The cold war was technically winding down, but they still didn't trust the Soviets. The CIA hated them. They knew the Soviets had a lot more clandestine stuff going on than we knew about, which they probably did. But spies and espionage are expensive. They wanted to know if there was another way, maybe even a faster and more effective way. So they started recruiting."

Dennis gave him a quizzical look. "But how did you get mixed up in all of it?"

"That was about the same time I had my car accident. I was twenty-three, driving home one night after work. A drunk driver hit me. Luckily it wasn't very fast because we didn't wear seat belts back then.

I still hit the windshield hard enough to give me a concussion. Dr. Rief treated me in the emergency room, but there weren't any symptoms to suggest it might be more serious. Two days later I had an episode, like Evan."

"What happened?"

"It was brief, the first time. But that's how they start. And they didn't happen as frequently with me as they are now with him. Eventually though, I started seeing things. I thought they were hallucinations and so did Rief when I told him about them. He wasn't all that worried. Apparently all kinds of strange things can happen following a concussion. He kept an eye on me though."

Taylor stopped briefly as if remembering something new. "He was actually more concerned about the frequency than what I was actually seeing. It wasn't until he suspected a more serious problem that he begun delving more into the images I had been describing."

"But he believed you then?"

Taylor almost scoffed. "You could say that. When I described his living room at home right down to his favorite painting, he became a believer."

Shannon nodded. "I can relate."

Taylor shrugged. "By then, I was having physical problems that were clearly related to the visions. Rief was getting more and more worried. He called everyone he knew, but no one had any idea what it was. Finally, he got desperate and submitted it to a medical journal. What we didn't know was that it was one of the sources that Bollinger and his other spooks used to look for so-called psychics. Rief had put in enough detail about my visions that the article caught the CIA's attention.

Up until then they'd been recruiting by posing as scientists and doctors. In fact, the night I was abducted, someone called Rief earlier in the day claiming to be a doctor from Washington, D.C. Evidently, they were going to recruit me just as they had the others, by offering me money to participate. But when Rief laid out what was happening to me and what I was able to do in detail, I guess they didn't want to take any chances."

So, what, they just grabbed you?"

"They just grabbed me."

"And no one knew?"

"Nope. At the time, I lived by myself. As far as I can tell, no one saw anything."

"Where did they take you?"

"Back to Langley. I was young and didn't know what the hell was going on. They used a lot of intimidation and accusations. Pretty soon I was ready to do whatever they asked just to clear myself. That's how the government does it. They overwhelm and scare the hell out of you."

"So you couldn't resist," offered Shannon.

"I couldn't have resisted even if I wanted to. The visions were happening all the time by then. It was better if I at least had some say in it." Taylor picked up the cup and finished the rest of his coffee. "I'll never forget the first time I did it for them. I'm pretty sure at least one of them pissed their pants."

Dennis and Shannon smiled simultaneously. "How did it happen?"

"They had one of their spooks sitting in the next room. A room I'd never been in. I was supposed to try to see the picture he'd drawn on a piece of paper."

Taylor actually smiled. "Instead, I read some the newspaper on the table next to him, word for word."

Dennis began to laugh but caught himself. "No bullshit?"

"No bullshit," Taylor answered, smiling. He looked out through the sliding glass door into the darkness beyond, and the smile faded. "You see, they never told you whether you were right or wrong. They figured too many wrong answers would damage the subject's confidence and skill. But *I* sure knew. They couldn't hide the look on their faces. Of course that was a big mistake. Everyone went nuts after that. But each time they had me do something harder, farther away. Pretty soon I realized I was in trouble. Both from them and from the symptoms. They knew they finally had a real 'remote viewer' but ironically, one who was slowly dying on them."

"I couldn't sleep anymore and with every vision I did for 'em, I was coughing up enough blood to dye my shirt. Their doctors tried everything to stop it. They gave me all kinds of drugs and injections, but it just made things worse. But it was the last vision I did for them that changed everything."

"The Russians had built a large complex in a remote section of Crimea, with hundreds of trucks going in and out. The CIA could see it from their satellite shots but couldn't figure out what they were doing inside. Even though my health was failing, they pushed me to 'view' it. And I did. When I told them what was inside, and gave them a way to verify it, that was it. That was the end."

Shannon raised her eyebrow. "The end of what?"

"The end of me. At least as far as they were concerned. They knew I was dying…and quickly.

But for the first time, they also knew they had someone with a provable ability. An ability that could allow them to see anything. For an intelligence agency, it was…godlike. And yet, I was about to die and take it all with me."

Taylor paused again and fell silent. His face took on a hard expression as the emotions behind the memories came flooding back.

"They didn't give a damn about me. They just wanted what was in my head. Or more importantly, to find out what was so unique about my brain. Even if they had to go in and find out."

Shannon gasped. "What? They were going to…"

"Operate." Taylor stared down at the table and shook his head. "If they couldn't save me, they decided to at least find out what it was that made my visions possible. And once I was dead it would be too late. They had to find out while I was still breathing."

"My God!" Shannon exclaimed, under her breath. She had a thought and tilted her head. "How did you know what they had planned?"

Taylor peered at her, sarcastically. "Are you joking?"

Dennis leaned forward, placing his elbows on the table. "And then?"

"I had to get out of there," Taylor said. "I did more during those tests than they knew. By then I'd *seen* their whole complex, where they met, where they worked, even the grounds outside. And I knew where the infirmary was. I also knew where the cameras were and where they weren't. So I faked a health scare. Course, in my case, I guess I wasn't much of a stretch. The last night there, I let my body

40

hemorrhage and just tried to keep myself breathing and alert. They freaked out and rushed me to the infirmary, and then called the surgical team. But I managed to recover enough to grab something heavy and hit the two spooks who were in the room with me. I got their keys and made it outside. Even grabbed one of their cars."

Dennis smiled. "You escaped."

"I escaped. Made it a couple hundred miles before running out of gas, but then I ditched the car and took off on foot. I wasn't able to move very fast in my condition, but I had enough of a lead that they never found me.

"Next morning I woke up in the woods, lost. It took me all day, but eventually I stumbled across a large house, which turned out to be a church. An old pastor took me in and cleaned me up." Taylor grinned. "Fortunately, he wasn't much of a fan of the government either. That man saved my life twice." Taylor looked up and saw both Dennis and Shannon waiting expectantly. "He helped me get to the train station bound for Montana. But I wouldn't have made it if he hadn't helped me with something else. I told him about what was happening to me. About the visions. He didn't understand it, but he did come up with what I needed to survive it."

"The cross?"

"That was one part of it," Taylor confirmed. "But it was the realization that wherever I was on the other side, I needed an anchor. Something to keep me here. Something to remind me how close I was to death and that I could not let myself be afraid." Taylor couldn't believe the memories were still so clear. "I'm not religious. The cross is symbolic, just

41

like the phrase from the Bible. What it's really about is staying grounded. Anchored. And providing yourself a way back."

Shannon gazed at him solemnly. "Are you going to be able to help Evan?"

As the last word rolled off her tongue, Shannon realized how afraid she actually was of Taylor's answer.

"I don't know. Maybe. But…" Taylor added before she looked too relieved, "that kid has a hard road ahead of him. He was expecting to fix this quickly. It's not going to be like that. I was serious when I said there is no *fix*. All he can do is endure it. Soon he'll need to accept that things will never be the same. His battle will last the rest of his life. And death will come when he can no longer resist.

"I learned to endure because I had more time. Evan's ability is stronger and how much he's able to stand is up to him." He looked at Shannon. "I think that's your department, Counselor."

Finally, Taylor checked his watch and slowly stood up. "I need to hit the sack."

Dennis stood up with him and extended his hand. Taylor reached out to shake it. He then nodded at Shannon and a sleeping Ellie and headed for the other room.

"Dan," Dennis said, stopping him. "Are you sure that guy Bollinger would still come after you?"

"He would if he knew I was alive."

"How do you know?"

At that, Taylor smirked. "Because when I escaped from that building, Bollinger was one of the two spooks I knocked out in the infirmary."

8

The early morning sun bathed the bedroom in a warm light, and the edge of its rays crept across the room. They eventually crawled across Evan's face, causing his eyes to flutter and open. He lay still for several minutes before finally sitting up in bed. With a grimace, he clutched a hand against his chest.

It had been almost two weeks now and the pain was still there. *God, would it ever go away?*

According to Dan Taylor, it wouldn't. Evan didn't want to believe that, but he was gradually accepting the reality that it wasn't getting much better. It was no longer getting worse, but it certainly wasn't getting better. At all.

It was excruciating, and at its worst in the morning. Even when it subsided somewhat throughout the day, he would still occasionally experience a sudden jolt of pain that would stop him in his tracks. Dan Taylor insisted that in time the frequency of the jolts would decrease, but so far, Evan hadn't noticed any change.

After a few relaxation techniques, he bent down and reached out gingerly to retrieve his pants. Then his shirt. He got dressed and quietly made his way downstairs.

As he neared the bottom of the stairs, he was only mildly surprised to see Ellie run into the room. She looked at him eagerly.

"Do you want to play catch?"

Evan grinned and palmed the large ball atop the end of the banister as he stepped onto the soft carpet. He had to acknowledge that this was his own doing. He'd been teaching Ellie to play catch with a softball.

"Sure," he replied. "Let me get my shoes."

The Mayer's backyard was large, balancing the size of the house. A playset sat idle in the far corner, across a wide stretch of yellow grass struggling to recover.

The two walked into the middle of the grass and stopped. Evan watched Ellie struggle only slightly with her glove this time before holding it out and grinning back at him. The two had been spending more time together as Evan worked through what Dan Taylor liked to call his "rehabilitation." He was pretty sure rehabilitation meant you were supposed to improve though.

Evan slipped on his own glove and tossed the green softball to Ellie. She missed and immediately ran after it. His lips curled with admiration. She was getting better.

After almost thirty minutes, Ellie decided she was done and ran to the playset. Evan followed and sat in the second swing hanging from a huge overhead beam, while Ellie swung back and forth next to him.

"You seem excited, Ellie."

She grinned again and continued pumping her legs. "My mommy said I can go back to school soon."

"Are you nervous at all?"

She cocked her head for a moment, thinking. "No."

"Good."

"How long are you going to stay with us?"

Evan looked back at the house. "I'm not sure. I

guess I still need to work some things out."

The young girl had a thought and stopped pumping. She straightened her legs and dragged herself to a stop. "Wait here," she said, before darting across the grass.

Evan watched her disappear into the house. He took a deep breath and looked up at the trees around him. The morning air felt fresh.

A few minutes later, Ellie bolted back out of the house, remembering to stop and close the sliding glass door behind her. She then bounded across the grass and back to her swing.

"Where did you go?"

She peered up at him with concern. "I heard my mommy and Mr. Taylor talking about how you need something to help you remember." She turned to him and opened her hand, revealing an oversized gold locket. She handed it to Evan. "You can use this. It helped me remember when I was with that bad man."

He looked down at her softly and picked the locket up out of her palm. He turned it over in his hand and then split the side open, revealing two pictures inside: one of Ellie's mother and one of her father.

"The bad man never found it because I kept it hidden."

Evan was overwhelmed. She was such a sweet girl. And full of surprises. "Thank you, Ellie. Thank you very much."

"You're welcome." With that, she leaned back and started swinging again.

"Am I interrupting something?"

With naturally wavy hair falling over her tanned shoulders, Tania was dressed attractively in shorts and a light-colored tank top. She and Evan had developed a strong relationship over the last few weeks after she watched him risk his own life to rescue Shannon's daughter, Ellie.

Only a year older than Evan, Tania had finally had enough with the shallow and materialistic guys that were constantly surrounding her. Instead, she found something remarkable in a slight, and somewhat shorter, guy. There was something in his character that she had never seen before at her age. Evan had more compassion and courage than any of the guys she'd met. To her, he was a diamond in the rough.

Evan turned and instantly rose from the swing when she spoke. "Uh, no."

"Hi, sweetie," Tania said, waving at Ellie, still swinging.

"Hi, Tania."

She watched Ellie for a moment before turning to Evan. "Am I too early for our walk?"

"Not at all."

Truth be told, it was Tania's visits during the week that were keeping Evan sane. She had a way about her that he couldn't quite describe. She was also beyond beautiful, which Evan wasn't entirely sure she was aware of. But even more than that, there was something about her disposition that he could feel. Her mere presence elicited a strange calming effect every time he was around her. Each walk they took together left him looking forward to the next.

But he wasn't sure how she felt about him. Was she just helping out given what he'd done for Dr.

Mayer? He doubted he was her type, but they *did* have amazing conversations. He talked with her about things he never thought anyone else thought about, certainly not at his age. If she were interested in anything beyond friendship, he couldn't tell. *Wouldn't the signs be more obvious? Sometimes she would touch him lightly on the arm, but did she do that with everyone?* If he said something and was wrong, it would be the kind of rejection he really didn't need right now. So he decided to say nothing.

After taking Ellie back inside, the two left through the front door and walked down the long driveway toward the street.

"You okay?"

"Yeah. I'm fine."

"Were you two having a moment back there?" she teased.

"Kind of."

"I think that's very sweet. I'm sorry I interrupted."

They reached the end of the driveway and let themselves out through a white metal gate.

"How about going to Montrose?"

"Sure." Evan didn't really care where they went. "I'll buy you some breakfast."

"I think it's my turn." His mood always lightened during their walks. And the walks were getting longer and longer. *That had to mean something, didn't it?*

"How's class?"

"Fine. It figures high school would finally get better *now*." He wished he'd made his changes a long time ago. Changes that could have helped him avoid his injury altogether.

"No kidding." Tania chuckled before reaching out and touching a flower as they passed a protruding bush. "Are you still feeling better?"

"I am. Thanks." It was a half-truth, which was close enough. He didn't want to add any unnecessary drama during their time alone. Especially when there wasn't much either of them could do about it.

"How was work?"

She shrugged. "Good. Although Dr. Mayer had a couple weird clients in today."

"Really? Weird how?"

"Well, one is a woman who's an obsessive compulsive. She's nice enough but watching her in the reception area is kind of an experience. She keeps a container of Clorox wipes in her purse and wipes down everything. The door handle, the chair, even the magazines."

"The magazines? How do you wipe down a magazine?"

"Very carefully," she smiled. "She doesn't do it every time but it's worth seeing when she does."

Evan looked puzzled. "Why would she only wipe down the magazines sometimes?"

"Yeah!" Tania laughed. "Like I'm going to ask her that."

"Good point."

"The other patient is a man who has an addiction to exercise."

"What?"

"Yeah. To exercise!"

"Is that even possible?"

"Sure, you can be addicted to anything."

Evan thought it over. "Is being addicted to exercise even a bad thing?"

"Well, it can be when it becomes a problem. He's been caught multiple times, running in place in the

48

bathroom at work."

This time he stopped and turned toward Tania. "Really?!"

She laughed again. "Really!"

Evan tried to imagine someone sneaking into a restroom to run. "Maybe my problem isn't so weird after all."

"That's what I've been trying to tell you." She grabbed his arm just below his short sleeve and pulled him forward playfully, continuing to walk. "You have to stop looking at this as a curse."

Easy for her to say. He hadn't quite told her everything yet.

"Okay, maybe curse is a strong word."

"Evan, you risked your life to save Ellie, even after you knew what it might do to you. I'm not kidding. You didn't save just one life, you saved three. You saved an entire family. It's not just about what happens to one victim, it's about everyone else it affects. With Ellie, it was more than just her. It was her parents, her aunt Mary, grandparents, friends at school. I told you about what happened to my aunt last year. When she died, a part of everyone around her died too. No one ever thinks about the ripple effects."

"I know. I guess it's just hard to remember sometimes."

"And it's not just that, Evan." Her hands were on her hips again.

"What do you mean?"

"I believe we all have a contribution to make in the world, no matter how small. Sometimes we know what it is and sometimes we don't. But imagine how terrible it would have been if Ellie's contribution just…disappeared, forever. I mean, what if she's supposed to do something amazing, like invent something, or be the President someday? You just never know. Imagine all the contributions that have been lost forever because kids disappear. And then someone like you comes along."

Evan stopped again. This time distracted by a blue car at a stop sign several yards away. In the back seat, he spotted the face of a special needs child. Curiously, he watched as the car pulled away with the child smiling and waving at him.

"What I'm saying," said Tania, "is that you can't save *everyone*. But you sure saved Ellie."

"I think a lot of that was coincidence."

"Are you sure about that?"

He stood, quietly staring at Tania for a long time.

She didn't know what he was thinking, but she *was* beginning to wonder how many more times she had to touch him before he got the hint.

9

Evan sat quietly at the Mayer's dining room table. He feigned interest as his mother and Dennis Mayer talked about politics and the country's increasingly divisible party lines. Leaning back in his chair and from under a furrowed brow, Dan Taylor abstained from the discussion.

Evan kept his eyes down on the table, thinking. A few minutes later, Shannon returned from putting Ellie to bed. She passed them all briefly at the table and turned on a baby monitor on the kitchen counter. Ellie was still having nightmares, but thankfully they were steadily subsiding.

She turned back to the table and pulled a chair out for herself. She sat silently, listening to the conversation. Shannon then turned and looked at Evan to her right, who appeared to be deep in thought. Shannon watched him for a few long minutes before speaking.

"Evan, are you alright?"

He snapped out of his trance and glanced up. The others at the table stopped and turned to look at him. "Yeah. Yeah, I'm fine."

"Is something on your mind?"

He instinctively began to shake his head but caught himself. "Um...sort of."

Shannon waited patiently.

Finally, Evan continued. "I've been thinking...about stuff."

"You mean about the episodes, honey?" Connie spoke up.

"Not really. Well kinda. That and about school."

"Did something happen?"

He shook his head. "No. I was actually thinking that...I'm gonna graduate in a couple weeks."

When he didn't continue right away, Shannon pressed forward in her chair. "Is there a problem, Evan?"

He leaned back in the chair, keeping his palms down in front of him on the table. "Not really. But I've been thinking about what's after this." He looked apprehensively around the table. "It's been almost a month, and Mr. Taylor has helped me a lot. I mean, it's not necessarily getting better but it's definitely not getting worse. And he said over time it should slowly begin to get at least a little better."

Taylor leveled his gaze at him. "I said *easier*, not better."

"That's what I meant."

Shannon raised an eyebrow. "Are you uncomfortable here, Evan?"

"No. No. Nothing like that."

"Are you thinking of leaving?"

"Not really-" he stopped himself. "Well, maybe. But not in the way it might sound."

Connie moved to a chair closer to her son. She was now seated directly across from Shannon. "What is it, Ev?"

"I guess I'm just wondering what I do now. I mean, what's next? It's not like this problem is going to go away. So, once I'm out of school, what then?"

Connie opened her mouth to speak, but not having an answer, merely closed it again. The fact was that she and Shannon Mayer had thought a lot about what came next for Evan. She wanted him to come back home with her. As far as they could tell, his symptoms *had* seemed to have plateaued. And even if they hadn't, if there were more surprises ahead, they lived closer to the hospital than the Mayers did. After that, they would take it one day at a time.

According to Taylor though, there was no way to really tell if things might get worse. All he could offer was that it would come down to what kind of person Evan was inside. A person's true character was only revealed under real duress. And while Evan had managed to survive until now, the real fight lay in the years ahead, not the weeks behind him.

"What do you think should happen next, Evan?" Shannon asked calmly.

It had been two days since his conversation with Tania. And he hadn't been able to stop thinking about it since. "Well," he cleared his throat, "I've been thinking, a lot." He paused, considering how to phrase the rest. "I guess what I'm thinking…is that…since I, you know, helped find Ellie. Maybe I could help some other kids."

It was the last thing anyone at the table was expecting to hear. Everyone's mouth dropped slightly as they digested Evan's words. Shannon instinctively placed her hand across her chest, genuinely moved.

Dennis Mayer's eyes softened as he stared at Evan in awe. After everything this boy had been through, emotionally and physically, not to mention the pain that still lay ahead, he wanted to try to help others.

Evan's eyes met Mayer's. "I mean, Mr. Mayer was

53

a police officer. There's probably other people that need help, right?"

Dennis had to keep from rolling his eyes. *Probably? That was the understatement of the year.*

"No," Taylor said flatly. He shook his head and crossed his arms. "Absolutely not."

Everyone, including Evan, looked at him with surprise.

"Huh?'

"It's a terrible idea."

"It is?"

"Yes. It is."

"But…"

Taylor cut him off. "Listen to me, boy. Surviving these episodes is one thing but instigating them is another. This is not some parlor trick. Any one of these episodes could be your last. I told you what really lies on the other side. No matter what you do, *it* will get closer and closer until it can reach you. The last thing you want to do is encourage it.

"And even if you can withstand it forever," Taylor raised his voice and leaned forward, "and given how strong this is in you, I'm not sure you can, but even if you do, this curse cannot be hidden. If you go out there trying to help people with it, it's going to draw attention to you damn quick. And believe me, that is attention you don't want!"

Shannon turned from Taylor and looked thoughtfully at Evan. Even as abrasive as he was, she had to concede Taylor's point. "He's right, Evan. It's a wonderful thought, but it's dangerous for you on multiple levels. We're not out of the woods with this yet."

Evan did not deflate. If anything, his resolve

seemed to strengthen slightly. "I don't know if I'll ever make it out of the woods. And even if I do, how many kids could be found between now and then?"

Shannon didn't let the smile out. But she marveled at what a remarkable kid he was. Such a quiet strength. With that, she merely turned and looked back at Taylor.

"You don't know what you're saying," he growled. "You don't know the type of people who will do anything to get what you have. You don't understand what they're capable of. I'm telling you, you don't want this attention."

Dennis spoke up. "You *would* attract attention, Evan. Probably a lot."

Taylor nodded in agreement, next to Dennis. "It's a nice idea, kid, but trust me, you'd bring trouble down on everyone around you. The worst kind."

Evan blinked and dropped his gaze to the table again, thinking. Finally, he rose up and said, "I really want to try."

Taylor threw up his hands and fell against the back of his chair. He turned to Shannon and pointed angrily at Evan. "You need to talk some sense into him, Counselor!"

Shannon was studying Evan again. She knew him well enough to recognize the look of determination on his face. She had seen it before. This was no longer a question or debate.

Shannon raised an eyebrow at Taylor. "And what would you suggest he do instead? *Hide?*"

Taylor's eyes widened at the insult, and he glared at her across the table.

What no one had noticed was Connie Nash sitting quietly to the right of Evan. Motherly instincts would normally have had her objecting from the outset, but she knew her son better than anyone. She immediately recognized the look in his eyes. It was not just determination. It was something more.

She knew there was another reason Evan was doing this. And she was the only other person in the room who could understand.

10

Anne Keyes stared around her living room with a sense of both hope and dread. It was eerily quiet as the morning sun began to rise into the sky, shining through her front window. Over the next few hours, it would begin its work, thawing the winter morning frost and warming the air to a near balmy fifty degrees.

Keyes glanced down at her watch again. It was 6:50 a.m. People would be arriving shortly. She was hoping for fifty this time but worried it would be far less. The numbers had dwindled rapidly over the last month. She couldn't blame them, at least not out loud. In her own mind, she herself battled between feelings of appreciation and disgust. Appreciation for those still dedicated to sticking it out and a secret—but guilty — disgust for the majority who didn't. *Who cared about the holidays?*

The large table behind her was covered with flyers. A smaller table against the wall supported several large canisters of hot coffee and stacks of paper cups. Next to the cups were four dozen donuts in pink boxes.

She hoped to be on the road by 8:00 a.m. sharp.

Twelve people. Twelve lousy people. That was all that showed up. Her sense of despair deepened as the clock closed in on eight o'clock. She knew from experience, most of those who were coming had already arrived. There wouldn't be many stragglers. It meant they would be lucky to cover a third the distance she had mapped out. She forced herself to ignore the frustration and remember that thirteen was better than one.

Keyes watched silently as the group chatted with each other, coffee cups still in their hands. She was suddenly overcome by a feeling of loneliness as she thought about her life now and everything she had to do, alone. The doorbell rang, and she shook herself out of it. *Fourteen is better than thirteen,* she mused.

Crossing the carpeted floor, she opened the white front door to find two people standing on her porch. She didn't recognize either of them.

"Good morning," she said, feigning a smile.

The larger of the two nodded. "Good morning. Are you Anne Keyes?" He already knew the answer.

"Yes, I am. Are you here to help?"

The dark-haired man raised an eyebrow and peered over her shoulder at the volunteers in her living room. "Oh, I'm sorry. We didn't realize you had company. We can come back another time."

Keyes looked at him curiously. "It's alright. I take it you're not here for the search?"

"No, ma'am."

"Oh," she frowned. "What can I do for you then?"

"My name is Dennis Mayer, from the L.A.P.D. We came to talk to you about your case."

Keyes' heart jumped. "Los Angeles Police? Did you find…"

Mayer raised his hand cautiously, cutting her off. "No, ma'am. I'm sorry, I didn't mean to imply that." He looked over her shoulder again. There was a brief look of reluctance on his face, but he relented. "Would you mind if we talked privately?"

Keyes asked one of her volunteers to go through the details of the search while she led her visitors to a small dining room on the other side of the kitchen.

"We're sorry. We can see you're busy," began Mayer. "But we wanted to talk to you about your daughter's case."

"Of course," she nodded, looking back and forth between them. "You just caught me a little off-guard. I didn't know LA was working on the case too."

"They're not officially," replied Mayer. "I'm retired. I'm more of a private investigator now, following a handful of special cases. Yours being one of them."

"I see," Keyes replied. "Well, I'm more than happy to answer any questions you have. I can use all the help I can get."

Mayer could hear the people in the other room and glanced around the corner before continuing. When he did, he lowered his voice. "We're familiar with most of the details regarding your daughter Katie. But there were a couple questions we wanted to ask you, things that generally take a while to be updated in the case file. First and foremost, has anyone been in contact with you? For example, a ransom note, a phone call, anything at all. It could even be something that struck you as odd but you assumed to be completely unrelated. Even a strange comment from a friend."

Keyes pondered the question. "No, nothing overt. And I'm trying to think of anything *odd* but nothing comes to mind. To be honest," she said with a longing look, "when you can't sleep for four months, your mind tries to connect anything and everything."

The truth was that Anne Keyes didn't know what to think. There were so many things about her daughter's disappearance that she couldn't understand. How could she just disappear less than eight blocks from her own house on a neighborhood sidewalk? How could no one have seen anything? Christ, most of the block knew each other; certainly by first name, if not by their last.

They lived in a very nice area, and Katie was twelve years old. She rarely walked home by herself, and even when she did, she knew what to do if approached by a stranger. The police thought that might mean Katie was abducted by someone she knew. But they'd checked everyone: family, friends…they'd even traced every person who had ever called or texted her phone.

Keyes shook her head, still thinking about the question. "I'm sorry, I can't think of a single thing."

"I understand." Mayer nodded sympathetically. "Just one last question. Do you know how many of those contacts — the people who called or texted your daughter's phone — did the police conduct a full background search on?"

"I'm not sure. Most of them, I think."

"I see," answered Mayer. He thought again about the group in her living room. He had counted twelve when they walked through. Keyes' numbers were falling fast. It was normal after a few months of searching. Most volunteers eventually got pulled away, having to attend to their own lives. It was understandable, but the obvious decline left the victim's family in an increasingly large emotional vacuum, lost in the void of loneliness and despair. *She did still have these twelve*, he thought, *and probably several more that couldn't make it that day.* But it didn't help that the mood was not an optimistic one.

Mayer could see the disappointment filling Anne Keyes' eyes as she realized her two visitors didn't know any more than she did. He finally bobbed his head slightly, turning and looking down past his right shoulder.

Evan was facing away from him, examining several photographs on a nearby shelf. His gaze finally circled back, and he looked up to Dennis Mayer. He then turned to Keyes and spoke quietly, for the first time. "Can we see her bedroom?"

11

The bedroom was large, much larger than the others he had been in. The expensive canopied bed stood against the far wall, which was mostly covered with posters; not altogether different from the others. He recognized several of the poster's bands, all popular among the middle school and high school crowds. In the middle was a thick pink and purple rug with an overly wide, half-height dresser stretched beneath the window in front of them. The space itself was immaculate.

Evan stepped to the middle and studied the room as he performed a three hundred and sixty degree scan. He paused on the closet, with its open door displaying the clothes inside. When he finished, he took a deep breath and nodded to Dennis.

Dennis turned to Keyes, who was standing pensively behind them. "Ms. Keyes. I need to ask you two things that may seem very unorthodox."

She cocked her head curiously. "Okay."

"First, I'd like to ask that you leave us alone in this room."

"Alone?"

"Yes."

Puzzled, she crossed her arms in front of her. "Why?"

"We would like to examine it more closely, privately."

"Privately?"

"That's right."

"For how long?"

"About thirty minutes."

"Well, we're supposed to leave. We're searching today and…"

"Stall."

"Stall?"

Dennis nodded. "I know this sounds strange, but we have some experience with this."

Keyes didn't understand. She glanced at Evan and then back at Dennis. "What are you going to do?"

"We just want to check things out. Try to see if the others missed anything."

"Okay." She was still hesitant, but frankly, she had nothing left to lose. Any possibility of finding a new clue, no matter how strange it might seem, was worth it.

She scanned the room one last time. "Can I…get you anything?"

Dennis looked to Evan who shook his head. "No, we're fine. But there's a second condition. Don't tell anyone about us. Not the people downstairs, not the other investigators, no one."

Keyes blinked, now even more confused. "Don't tell anyone?"

"That's right. No one. No matter what."

"Why?"

"We don't have time to explain. But I promise that if we can help, we will. If you keep it quiet. And I don't mean just for now, I mean forever."

Keyes remained still, staring at both of them. She had no idea what was going on. Who was the boy and why wouldn't an ex-policeman want anyone to know about them? She was utterly confused, but after a long silence, her exhaustion won out. She was so weary, both emotionally and physically, that she decided if these two wanted to remain anonymous, then she didn't really care. If they could help her, she was willing to do anything, and if they couldn't, then she had nothing to lose by forgetting they were ever there. At least she hoped that was true.

"Fine," she sighed. "You weren't here. But what am I supposed to tell the people downstairs?"

"Tell them we're investigators that needed to verify a few things and leave it at that."

Keyes nodded. "Thirty minutes?"

This time Evan spoke up. "Maybe less."

Evan stood motionless in the middle of the room, which had now become deathly quiet. With the door closed, he and Dennis could no longer detect even the low murmur of voices downstairs. Evan was struck by how different each of the kids' rooms had been, and yet again how similar.

It had been over four months now, and this was the fourth family the duo had visited. Together they had found three more children. The first two were still alive, miraculously, but unfortunately the third was not. The emotional collapse of realizing the young boy was deceased was something Evan was not ready for. In fact, the sudden emotional change on the "other side" weakened him considerably, and he nearly lost his link — his anchor — back to the world of the living.

They eventually found the boy's body, which the family was still grateful for, but Evan wasn't sure if he would ever be the same after that single moment. He realized he was going to have to learn a way to somehow brace himself for that next eventuality.

It was easier to think about the two other girls they had saved. One had been kidnapped and kept in a shed amid a fairly populous neighborhood. The kidnappers, a man and his wife, held her for years and had her so brainwashed that the girl almost didn't want to be rescued.

The second girl, even younger, was recently kidnapped by her deranged father. The crime was not a mystery, but where they had fled to was. The father was constantly on the move, but eventually they found them.

In each instance, all three families swore themselves to secrecy over Evan and Dennis' participation. A promise they both made to Dan Taylor, and the necessary level of caution to keep Evan safe.

They waited until they could approach the families quietly and eventually swore them to silence.

And yet, through all of the work, the most gratifying part of it all was being present when the families were reunited with their child. Even in death. The outpouring of emotion was simply indescribable. The realization that they had been given another chance to hold their child in their arms meant more to them than life itself. Two of the fathers had fallen onto their knees and wept. Those were moments that Evan would remember for the rest of his life.

But now, as he stood in the middle of Katie Keyes' bedroom, he began to grow nervous. Would he experience the despair of finding her *beyond help*, and if so, would it cause him to lose his grip again?

"You okay?" Dennis asked.

"I think so."

Evan moved gingerly to the girl's bed. He ran two fingers lightly over the smooth sateen sheets. After a long moment, he turned around and eased himself onto the side of the mattress. With another look at Dennis, he turned and raised his legs up. He then lowered his head onto the pillow.

As he looked up at the canopy above him, he thought he could still detect the scent of the girl's shampoo on the pillow. He lowered his arms to either side with fists down and tried to relax. The pills in his mouth were nearly dissolved, and he opened his right hand to look at the object inside. It was the locket Ellie had given him. Evan rubbed a thumb over it lightly before turning it sideways and popping it open. Inside were two pictures: one of his little sister and the other his father.

With a deep breath, he closed his eyes.

12

It took longer to feel it, but the coolness eventually came. It washed over him in the darkness like a powerful wave, sending chills through his body. He remained motionless, waiting.

In the distance, the blackness began to grow lighter until it eventually coalesced into a tiny dot. The small light seemed to freeze for a moment before exploding wider and rushing toward him. He braced his body for the impact, but there was no particular feeling when it overtook him and surrounded his body in bright, white light.

Evan could sense himself thinking, almost as if he could feel the electrical signals traveling through his brain. He couldn't tell if it was real.

One surprise that he wasn't expecting was that, during every episode, his entrance to the other side was never the same. Sometimes faster, sometimes slower. And the fog. The fog was always different. Always moving.

The space immediately before him began to swirl into the shape of a large tunnel. The rest of the fog twisted around in snaking patterns until small circles appeared deep in the mist.

Evan squeezed tighter. He could sense the sharp tip of the metal locket in his hand. This would not last long.

The circles then began to open, revealing the deep red ocean behind them.

Suddenly, there it was. The dread. The feeling of sickness and poison surrounding him. He could almost feel Death sensing his presence. It could sense his beating heart and crept closer through the fog.

Evan tried to visualize the picture sitting atop Katie Keyes' dresser. A picture of her young face, alive and smiling into the camera.

He pressed his eyes tighter, concentrating. The largest, tunnel-shaped hole continued growing in the fog in front of him, stretching until something became visible on the other side.

Evan stared hard into the swirling passageway and tried somehow to will himself just a little closer, but couldn't. He remained. Staring from a distance.

He could see images forming inside. He pressed forward again, straining to see. Someplace dark with a small light and...a shape.

Then it arrived. The terror. A sudden jolt coursed through his body, causing the muscles in his chest to seize violently.

Dennis Mayer knelt next to Evan, carefully watching the movements of his body: the chest and diaphragm for breathing abnormalities and his head for perspiration. Shannon's sister, Mary, had taught Dennis the signs to look for, in spite of Dan Taylor's insistence that only Evan could now return himself from out of the fog. Dennis didn't know if that was true, but if he saw Evan struggling, he was going to try whatever he could.

He jumped when Evan's body began spasming, nearly causing Dennis to fall backward. He quickly leaned forward and found Evan's wrist with his fingers. His pulse had quickened considerably. He checked the boy's forehead. Small beads of sweat had appeared.

Suddenly, Evan's body arched above the bed and all the muscles from his legs to his jaw tightened.

"Evan!" Dennis said aloud. After no response, he

leaned in closer. "EVAN!"

Evan tried to control the panic within his body. He scrambled to focus and forced himself to remember why it was happening. What exactly it was that was frightening his system.

He released all his energy from both the tunnel and its images. It was now about him.

"As I walk through the valley of the shadow of death..."

"EVAN!" Dennis shook him hard. He reached down and wrapped his hands around Evan's fists. He squeezed hard and forced the sharp point of the locket deeper into Evan's soft palm.

Evan's body bucked one last time and then became still. Dennis waited nervously. He was already reaching for his phone when Evan managed to open his eyes and immediately rolled to the side.

Dennis instantly grabbed a large plastic bag he had laid on the floor. He got it to Evan's mouth just in time for the teenager to vomit inside.

Once he was done, Evan rolled back onto the bed. Dennis reached out with a cloth and gently wiped his mouth. Evan looked up at him gratefully.

Dennis twisted the bag closed and stared at him. "Are you okay?"

"It's different when you *try* to make it happen." After only a brief moment, he quickly turned to Dennis.

"She's alive!"

13

They couldn't tell Anne Keyes what Evan had seen. Not yet. It was too soon, and while Evan was sure her daughter was alive, it still wasn't clear where she was.

The room that Evan had seen was dark, almost pitch black, with only a few hints of light. The walls seemed like concrete. The girl was lying down on some kind of a thin bed or cot. She wasn't moving on the bed, but she *was* breathing.

The room felt long, or wide, with strange sounds echoing from multiple directions. But Evan had not been able to make any of it out clearly before losing his connection to her.

Though tempted to give her some hope, they had to refrain from telling Keyes. They couldn't risk the possibility of her flying into hysterics, wanting to know how to find Katie. They needed her calm.

Instead, they simply told her they had some ideas but needed to return later, preferably when there were no other guests in the house. Keyes was still confused but agreed to let them back in that evening.

Evan wasn't done.

When the two left the house and walked to the curb, neither noticed the white car parked two houses down on the opposite side of the street. Inside the old Ford, on the driver's side, sat a lone figure. He was slouched down low in the front seat, peering just above the steering wheel and watching both of them climb into Mayer's large, gray truck.

Darias Black lowered his camera and checked the pictures he had just taken. He knew who Mayer was, but it was the first clear shot he'd gotten of the kid. Probably not much taller than five foot six with sandy-blonde hair. He was skinny and walked as if he was hurt, or maybe sick.

Black had been following Mayer for nearly a week. It took some effort to find out who was behind the recently solved abduction cases. For some reason, the newspapers did not cite a particular investigator behind them. In fact, they didn't report any significant details on the recovery of the children at all. Instead, there were just references to existing police investigations and "clues previously overlooked." They never actually said *who* had uncovered the new information.

It took Black a long time to find out. And it had to be done in a way that wouldn't tip off anyone on the other end of the phone.

Eventually, the person he was looking for turned out to be a man named Dennis Mayer, a recently retired cop from Los Angeles. He'd retired just months before, and quite coincidentally, after the surprising rescue of his own missing daughter. But now, instead of retiring, the detective appeared to be continuing his work in private. Miraculously, he seemed to be instantly successful at finding lost children. And he seemed to be doing so all by himself and covering his tracks for some strange reason.

But now Black knew the detective was not acting

alone. He looked to be working with a teenage kid who had not been identified in any of the news clippings or mentioned by anyone during his search to find Mayer. *But why?*

He continued examining the pictures on his digital camera and zoomed in on one of the better shots of the teenager. In the photo, Mayer was keeping his hand close to the kid as they walked. *Was he sick?* Mayer didn't have to help him get into the truck, but he was clearly weak.

So, how was this kid involved?

They appeared to be operating in secret, or at least in a manner meant to avoid attention.

Any other observer probably wouldn't think twice about the duo. Why would they? It took someone else, someone like Black, to know why. Either they didn't want anyone to know how they were finding lost kids or who was behind it. And if one of them was easily identifiable, meaning Mayer, then the person he was trying to hide was the teen. The boy was somehow involved in finding those children.

Black had finally found his targets.

The news of the first child being discovered had escaped his attention, but it was the second rescue that caught Black's eye; from a discarded newspaper on his bus. Of course, he never cared about the children. He just needed to know *who* was finding them.

It wasn't until the body of the young boy was found that alarm bells went off.

Darias Black didn't know how this teenage kid was helping Mayer, but he worried that if left alone they would eventually stumble upon a case that Black followed very, very carefully.

72

One that would lead Mayer and the kid directly to him.

14

That evening, Dennis and Evan returned to the Keyes house just after 9:00 p.m. An hour well after dark, and one that would put most neighbors already at home.

The night air was cold enough to make their breaths visible as they walked up the ornate stone path toward the front door. The porch light was off as requested, and Mayer quietly opened the screen door, knocking gently. A few moments later, Anne Keyes turned the deadbolt from the other side and opened the door.

"Hello," she said. She peered past them to the empty street before stepping back. "Please come in."

"Thank you." Mayer stepped in first, followed by Evan. When the door was closed, he turned to face Keyes. "We appreciate your flexibility."

She nodded. "I have to admit, I don't really understand what you're doing. But I'm not in much of a position to ask questions, am I?"

On the other hand, Keyes had done her research. She had called the L.A.P.D. that afternoon and confirmed that Mayer had, indeed, recently retired from the force.

"I can't imagine what clues you could be looking for in my daughter's room that the other officers haven't found. Or why you want to be alone in there. Please tell me you don't have some weirdo thing going on."

Dennis smiled. "No ma'am. We're not weirdos. Unorthodox maybe, but not weirdos."

Evan looked at Dennis but said nothing. He wasn't sure that was entirely true.

Keyes gave a tired sigh and shrugged. She turned and headed back up the stairs with Evan and Dennis following. She really *didn't* have much choice. She was both exhausted and desperate, and the case was cooling, still with no leads. Keyes had not heard anything from the Bakersfield Police Department for over two weeks which was not a good sign. People were losing hope and it was beginning to feel as though she was the only one trying to keep things going. More than anything else, she didn't know how many more times she could wake up in the morning with nothing but despair left in her heart.

Keyes pushed open the door to Katie's room and walked in. She stopped in the middle and turned toward Evan and Dennis. In a resigned tone, she stated, "I presume you need to be alone again."

Dennis frowned. They both knew how strange the request sounded. "Please."

"Fine." She passed them on the way out and, not saying another word, closed the door behind her. Without looking back, Keyes walked quietly to the top of the stairs and descended. Once in the living room, she sat down stoically on her couch and hung her head. The tears came easily and she wept, alone.

Twenty minutes later, Evan managed to push himself up and keep steady on the edge of the girl's bed. The sickness wasn't as bad tonight, but two visions in one day left him with barely enough energy to sit up. The episodes were now happening every day, whether he liked it or not. But eliciting them on purpose took a much larger toll.

Dennis put a firm hand on his shoulder as Evan suddenly wavered. "Easy."

Evan acknowledged weakly with a nod. "I saw...tunnels."

"Tunnels?"

"Big tunnels. Wide. And dark."

"Do you know where?"

"In a large city."

"How large is large?"

Evan shrugged. "I'm not sure. Big, like L.A. maybe."

"Los Angeles?" Dennis thought it over. "Which direction?"

"East, I think."

"How far east?"

"I'm not really sure. I couldn't see any names or signs, but there were a lot of buildings. And lots of lights."

"Do you know where these tunnels are?"

"Yes. If we can find the city, I can find the tunnels."

Dennis remained kneeling but raised one knee, resting his arm across it. "Okay. So it's a big city east of here. How many of the buildings were you able to make out? Were any noticeably taller than the others? Maybe lettering on it or a unique shape?"

Evan nodded his head slowly, as if it were still hurting. "Yes. There was a big building, shaped like a giant pyramid. And it had a bright light on top."

Anne Keyes quickly wiped her eyes and stood up when she saw Dennis helping Evan down the stairs.

"My God, what happened?!" She started forward until Dennis held up his hand.

"It's okay. We're fine." He kept an arm under Evan's until they reached the bottom. He spotted a rocking chair positioned across from the couch and helped Evan lower himself down into it.

Keyes stepped forward, concerned. "Are you alright?"

Evan nodded gratefully. "Yes ma'am."

Keyes eyed Dennis. "What on earth happened?"

He took a breath and leveled his gaze at her. "Ms. Keyes, I think you're going to want to sit down."

"What for?"

"Please." Dennis motioned to the couch behind her.

Apprehensively, Keyes moved backward and sat down on the white, leather couch. She peered past him to Evan as she kept trying to figure out what could have happened upstairs.

Dennis sat down on the end of the couch. "Ms. Keyes, we need to talk."

"About what?" No sooner had she finished the question than her eyes suddenly grew wide. "Wait. Did you find something?!"

He raised both hands in a cautionary gesture. "Before I say anything, I want to remind you of our agreement."

"You found something! What is it?"

"Not yet. First, you need to remember our deal."

"Yes, yes. I remember. Not a word to anyone."

"Not a word to anyone, *ever*." Dennis corrected.

"Yes, of course. No one."

"No matter who comes asking. No matter how many years later. You don't remember either of us."

"Yes! Alright! I promise. Now tell me, what did you find?!"

Dennis spoke calmly. "We can't tell you what we found. Instead, we'd like to tell you something much more important. At least for the moment." He took a deep breath. "We believe strongly that your daughter, Katie, is alive."

Keyes suddenly gasped, covering her mouth with her hands. "What?!"

"Alive," Dennis repeated.

She sat frozen on the couch. Her erect posture made it look as though she was about to leap up at any moment. But she didn't move. It felt like she was about to go into shock. Her arms began to tremble. "Alive," she whispered. "Are you sure?"

Dennis glanced at Evan, who was watching Keyes. "We're pretty sure."

She suddenly stopped. "How sure?"

"Very sure," Evan replied, from his chair.

Keyes looked at him and opened her mouth to speak but stopped again. She looked at the stairs and visually followed them up. "Wait. What happened to you upstairs? What exactly did you find?"

"Well, it's not so much what we found." Dennis tilted his head and briefly closed an eye, thinking how best to phrase it. "It's...kind of..." After a pause, he exhaled. "Different."

Keyes watched him as he spoke, and then turned to study Evan. He was still resting weakly. "Wait a second," she said. "Please don't tell me this is some kind of psychic thing."

"Well, not really," Dennis shrugged. "But…sort of."

The excitement instantly drained from her face. It was replaced by a pained, almost agonizing expression. "Oh my God," she said, visibly deflating in front of them. "You don't actually know anything. You're just guessing."

Dennis frowned. No, they weren't guessing, but how does one explain to someone else that they're not a kook? That what they could see, what Evan could see, was not what most people might envision.

A devastated Keyes slumped back into the couch with hands over her face. "That's why you didn't want me to tell anyone. Why you don't want anyone to know."

"No. That's not it."

She didn't hear him. She was already shaking her head. She was still reeling from the emotional plunge. It was her own fault. She had let herself get excited over someone having a *feeling* that Katie was still alive. *Was this how utterly desperate she had become?*

Keyes dropped her hands and stood up, exasperated. "Please leave," she said quietly.

Dennis and Evan looked at each other again.

"Ms. Keyes…"

"Thank you for trying to help," she cut him off. "But please, just go."

Outside, both Evan and Dennis stood watching as Anne Keyes closed both the screen and then the door in front of them.

With Dennis' arm still under his, Evan looked up at his partner's darkened figure. "That didn't go very well."

"No, it didn't." Dennis continued staring at the square shadow of the front door. "But maybe it's for the best."

Telling the parent what they knew was a risk. They knew that. It was intended to calm the person, to give them hope while Dennis and Evan then tried to find the child. But it could just as easily create a larger problem. Grieving parents were in a very unstable emotional state. A state that could explode in any direction, something Dennis Mayer knew too well. Sometimes the parent was on the cusp of doing something drastic, even if they didn't realize it. Therefore, giving the parents hope and putting an end to the anguish was the first step. Yet, while they knew it was a risk, this was the first time they hadn't made it past step one.

Dennis could understand Keyes' reaction. Trying to put your faith in the unknown wasn't easy when it was practically all you had left. Especially in some kid she'd never met before.

He looked down at the teenager who barely reached his shoulder. What she didn't know, however, was that Evan had not been wrong yet.

Darias Black silently scanned the street one last time. There were no cars approaching and no one was visible on either of the two sidewalks. His face was painted black to match his sweatshirt, pants, and dark shoes. His black hair made a cap unnecessary.

He reached down and fingered the small Glock, reassuring himself that it was still tucked inside his waistband. He was surprised that Mayer and the kid had come back so soon, but more than that he was thrilled at the opportunity it provided him. Their obsession over stealth was now his advantage. The darkness would make it easy to get close, and if he was fast enough, no one would see a thing.

He started his approach to the house discreetly while Dennis and the kid stood in front talking. He moved in a straight line, keeping a large tree in the neighbor's yard in between them to hide as much of his movement as possible.

His pace was quick. He reached down, wrapping his hand around the butt of the gun, and snaked a finger over the trigger. In one smooth movement, he slid it up and out from his pants.

If he was anything, he was methodical. A stickler for detail. It was how he had avoided capture thus far, even after multiple murders. He had to think of everything: every detail, every contingency, and every variable that might be out of his control.

As he approached the large tree, Black's entire shape disappeared behind it. He glanced thirty yards further down the street to his Ford, which was parked along the curb. It wasn't far beyond Keyes' house. He would be able to get to it quickly.

Black paused briefly at the sound of the television through the window of a neighbor's house he was passing. It sounded like some singing show. Inside, the owner would never notice Black moving across his own front lawn.

Now at the wide tree trunk, he glanced around the edge to see if his targets had moved from the next house's front porch. They hadn't.

The moment was in his favor, and he didn't hesitate. Black instantly rounded the tree and broke into a run, sprinting toward them at full speed.

"You need to get some rest."

Evan shook his head at Dennis Mayer's silhouette. "I can rest as you drive. We need to get to her daughter."

The kid was right. There was no way to know how much time Katie Keyes had left, or what condition she was in. But with any luck they would be back in Bakersfield with Katie in a couple days.

"Okay, let's get going then." He turned and led Evan down the stone steps toward the sidewalk.

Evan took only a single step before he suddenly gasped. A paralyzing jolt passed through him and his body went rigid. It caused him to stumble, tripping against the edge of the next stepping stone. He tried to reach for Dennis' hand, which had slipped out from under him, but missed.

The last thought Dennis had before spinning around was how odd an old car nearby looked, parked in that upscale neighborhood. But now he was moving, clutching after Evan, who was gasping and falling away from him. He never saw the dark figure appear behind him.

Luck was on Darias Black's side. He'd managed to make it across both front yards without a sound. Better yet, as he reached Mayer and the kid, their silhouettes actually appeared to be turned away from him.

He didn't stop running. He didn't even slow down. Instead, he passed less than fifteen feet away and fired two rounds just as the teenager appeared to trip and fall.

Black never broke stride. After his two shots, he continued past them at full speed and straight for his car.

15

Bright flashes accompanied by two earsplitting explosions startled them both, as Evan fell to the ground and Dennis fumbled to grab him.

Suddenly, Dennis' motion changed and his twisting body accelerated, missing Evan's outstretched hand. Evan hit the ground first, followed by Dennis whose motion sent him spinning out of control until he lost his balance. He fell with a heavy thud onto the edge between the stone and grass and rolled hard into Evan.

When Dennis realized what had happened, it took only seconds for him to retrieve his own gun and jump up onto his knees. He sighted the dark figure as it reached the car he'd noticed at the next house, but he couldn't see well enough to fire a shot.

If he missed, the bullet from his gun wouldn't stop until it hit a nearby house. And a forty-five caliber round had more than enough power to go through multiple layers of stucco and drywall.

Black reached his car in less than ten seconds, with the keys already in his hand. He yanked the door open and jumped in behind the wheel. Careful not to touch the brake pedal, he turned the ignition and pressed his foot onto the accelerator. The engine roared to life.

Black dropped the transmission down three

notches and eased off the gas to keep from peeling out. Leaving the headlights off would allow him to get away with the least amount of attention. Some neighbors might still notice the shape of a white car leaving the scene, but without its lights on, they would have a difficult time identifying the make and model.

After pulling away, he tightened his grip and pressed harder against the pedal, feeling the car quickly accelerate. It was over. Now he just had to get as far away as possible. Even if he hadn't killed both of them, killing just one would likely be enough to stop their investigations.

In an instant, Black noticed something out of the corner of his eye but it happened too fast. Something moved on the other side of the street. A car. No, a truck leapt away from the curb and careened into the left side of Black's Ford as he passed. The impact was immense, and the truck didn't stop. Instead the driver continued to ram right through him, almost pushing the Ford to the other side of the street.

From behind the wheel of the truck, Dan Taylor yelled to Tania across the front seat. "You okay?!"

She raised her head and looked around, dizzily. "Yeah."

"Stay here!"

Taylor threw open the driver's door and jumped out. He ran straight for the car that was now wedged sideways against the curb. Black struggled behind his own wheel, repeatedly smashing the accelerator to the floor in an effort to break the entanglement. He had no way to know from his position that his car's left rear wheel was virtually destroyed and protruding sideways from under the fender like a broken limb.

The rear axle had been completely sheared.

Black repeatedly floored the gas pedal, desperate to escape. The engine was roaring and the Ford's remaining rear wheel was spinning, but it was not enough to break away.

Darias Black's eyes widened when he saw a large frame appear at his window. Black hadn't realized his side window was broken until the other man's giant fist came through, striking the side of his head. He tried to raise his arm to block the second punch, but whoever was outside his car now had a chance to secure his footing. The second strike was even harder, and it was the last thing Black saw before he lost consciousness.

"Evan!" Dennis reached down and grabbed him by the shoulders. Evan seemed dazed with his eyes only half open. In the darkness, he quickly searched the teenager, feeling for any spots that might be wet with blood.

When he heard the collision, Dennis stopped and looked up. Taylor and Tania had been waiting in his truck down the street. And it looked like they had just plowed directly into the bastard as he tried to flee. Dennis watched Taylor's giant silhouette get out and rush to the side of the old car before he turned his attention back to Evan.

"Are you hurt? Do you feel any pain?" Dennis continued patting him down, searching.

Evan did not answer. Instead, he mumbled something as he tried to regain his bearings. Dennis felt around until he found the front zipper and unzipped the sweatshirt. He snaked his hand inside and over Evan's T-shirt. All dry.

"Evan, can you hear me?!"

From the ground, he nodded and spoke with a hoarse voice. "Yes."

"Are you hurt?

Evan blinked. "I'm not sure."

Dennis reached down and gripped Evan's hand, gently pulling him up into a sitting position.

"What happened?"

Dennis didn't answer. He was instead now examining his own left arm, which was bleeding badly. He winced and ripped his shirt sleeve open around the wound, before rotating his arm slowly. A gash cut across most of his outer tricep. He couldn't tell how deep it was in the darkness, but he could clearly make out blood. A lot of it.

When Evan spotted the wound, he gasped. He quickly unzipped and removed his sweatshirt, handing it to Dennis.

Dennis wrapped the garment around his arm and cinched it as tight as he could.

"How bad is it?!" Taylor asked, upon reaching them. He bent down and put his face close to Evan's, trying to see him. "You alive, kid?!"

"Yeah, I'm okay. It's Mr. Mayer who's hurt."

Taylor looked to Dennis when Anne Keyes' porch light came on and blinded them. They both squinted at her door as the screen was pushed open. "What was that?!"

Taylor glared at Dennis and spoke under his breath. "We've got to get Evan out of here! Now!"

Dennis looked up to see more lights coming on across the street, and some of the neighbors peering out from their living room windows.

"Go! Take him!"

Taylor didn't wait for another word. In two seconds, he had Evan's small frame up and over his shoulder. He turned and immediately withdrew from the area lit up by Anne Keyes' porch light. It took less than twenty yards for Taylor and Evan to disappear completely into the darkness.

Dennis placed a hand on his knee to help himself up and winced again. When he turned, Keyes suddenly gasped in panic.

"You're hurt!" She looked closer at his arm. "My God, were you shot?!"

"Yes. Call the police and tell them there was a shooting at your address." He peered at the shadow of the old car still attached to his truck. "And tell them the suspect has been in a car accident but is still armed."

Dennis tried to hold his arm steady as he ran to the car. The slightest move of his muscles was becoming excruciating. When he arrived, the passenger door on his truck swung open and Tania's petite frame jumped down.

"I'm okay!"

Dennis nodded and continued to the car's driver door which was almost wrapped around the truck's grill. Whoever was inside was out cold, lying across the front seat.

He quickly turned to Tania, who approached behind him.

"Tania, listen to me very carefully."

16

"What happened?!" Mary asked, frantically. She opened Shannon's passenger door and jumped inside the BMW.

"I don't know!" Shannon stomped on the gas, causing the door to slam shut behind her sister. As she sped away, Shannon checked the rearview mirror to see Ellie sitting quietly behind them.

The seatbelt alarm sounded from the dashboard and Mary twisted around. She pulled it quickly across her body, fastening it as Shannon sped down the car-lined street.

"Dennis said there was an incident and we needed to get there fast."

"Is Evan hurt?"

"I'm not sure. They're not together. He didn't have much time to talk. He said the police were coming."

Mary's eyes opened wide. "The police?!"

Shannon nodded and slowed, turning right onto a cross street and accelerating again.

"What happened with the police? Do they have Evan?"

"I don't think so."

"Then where is he?"

"I don't know, Mary! They're still somewhere in Bakersfield. Dennis said something happened and we needed to hurry. He said he'd call me again as soon as he could."

89

Shannon reached the on-ramp to the 210 Freeway and sped up the small grade. Thankfully, L.A. traffic lightened at night. She crossed into the third lane and stayed carefully behind another car. It was painful for her not to go any faster, but she could almost hear Dennis preaching to her. *Don't be the fastest car on the road. You'll stand out.*

She gripped the wheel with both hands. The last thing they needed now was to be stopped by the Highway Patrol.

Bakersfield was just over a hundred miles away, which at their speed meant roughly ninety minutes. It was at precisely forty-two minutes into their drive that Shannon's phone rang. Mary didn't wait for permission from her sister. She immediately picked it up and answered.

"Hello?"

"Who's this?"

"Mary."

"This is Taylor." After a slight pause, he continued. "I've got Evan. We need a ride."

"Is he okay?"

"Yes."

"Thank God. Hold on." Mary opened the glove compartment, searching for a pen and something to write on. "Where are you?"

"We're at a Starbucks on Panama. Where are you?"

"On the freeway. We're about forty-five minutes away. What's going…"

"Hurry," was all Taylor said before hanging up.

Mary looked at the phone and watched the call

end. "Well, that was abrupt."

"Where are they?"

"At a Starbucks." Mary opened an application on the phone and began typing in the street name. "He said Evan's okay."

"What else did he say?"

Mary replied sarcastically, "I think he said to hurry."

Shannon rolled her eyes. "That's it?"

"Pretty much."

They were there in thirty-eight minutes.

Shannon swerved into a mostly empty lot and nearly screeched to a stop in front of the store. Mary barely had her door open before both Taylor and Evan exited the store. Taylor had an arm around Evan, helping him move quickly to the car, while Mary rushed back to open the rear passenger door.

Shannon peered at her daughter through the mirror again. "Ellie. Scoot over, honey."

The young girl unbuckled and hastily slid behind her mother, making room.

Evan managed to climb in and pull himself across the seat, next to Ellie. He smiled weakly at her and winked. Mary followed him in. She flipped on the car's interior light above them and leaned his head back to assess his condition.

"What happened, Evan?"

"Someone found him," growled Taylor. "That's what happened." He climbed into the front next to Shannon and slammed the door closed. "Get us the hell out of here!"

Shannon backed up and tore out of the parking

lot. "What happened? Where's Dennis and Tania?"

"We don't know."

In the back, Mary examined Evan's eyes. She then switched to checking his pulse, which felt normal. "How do you feel, Evan?"

He thought for a moment. "Like a suitcase in one of those commercials."

She grinned and placed her hand against his forehead. A little warm but nothing alarming. "So is someone going to tell us what happened or not?"

He shook his head. "I don't know. We were leaving Ms. Keyes' house and something happened. It was like a bright flash in my head and then my legs just kinda fell out from under me. I thought maybe it was a seizure."

"Any idea what caused it?"

"No. That's all I saw. Then I was on the ground and heard the gunshots."

"GUNSHOTS?!" Shannon nearly slammed on the brakes. She managed to slow the car and pull over. She turned back to look at Evan. "There were gunshots?!"

Taylor frowned. "Yes."

"My God, was anyone hurt?!" Her mind immediately raced to Dennis, and then Tania.

"Your husband was hit in the arm. It didn't look too serious."

Oh God. "How serious is 'serious'?"

"A wound on his arm," Evan offered from the back seat. "He tied it up and told us to get out of there."

Shannon turned back around and stared through the front windshield. "Jesus. Please tell me he's on his way to the hospital."

"He's on his way to the hospital," Taylor lied. He then nodded to the steering wheel. "Now let's go."

"We need to call him!"

"No, we don't," argued Taylor. "We need to get out of here right now."

"But…"

Taylor cut her off. "Listen to me! Both of you. Someone found out about him. I don't know who they are or how they did it, but now they know who Evan is. They know *what* he is." He turned around and looked for anyone behind them. "If you want to protect Evan, you'll get him out of here right now!"

The women glanced at each other through the mirror and Shannon relented. She needed to know what happened, but this wasn't the time or place. Besides, she reasoned, if Dennis were really hurt badly, either he would have said something or Tania would have already called her back.

"Fine." She looked over her left shoulder and pulled back out.

Taylor turned forward, watching the road from under his heavy brow. They were moving and that's all he cared about. He was afraid, and it wasn't just for Evan. He was worried about something bigger. *If someone had found Evan, maybe they had found him too.*

17

From its original founding in 1898 with only a single marshal, the Bakersfield Police Department had since grown to more than four hundred officers and staff, covering an impressive one hundred and thirty square miles. Ironically, after notable milestones in its history — such as the first female officer in 1941, and less than three decades later, the first African-American officer — the city had recently come under public scrutiny over accusations of heavy-handed tactics and overuse of force. It was an image that Bakersfield was trying hard to change.

Dennis Mayer noted the single gold bar on each side of the officer's dark blue shirt collar when he entered the rather nondescript office. The man was a lieutenant, and by Dennis' estimation, probably the highest ranking officer in the south side substation at that hour.

Dennis watched as the officer lowered himself onto the edge of the desk, facing him. On his right breast pocket was a small, rectangular nameplate emblazoned with the name "Patrick."

"Good evening, Mr. Mayer. I'm Lieutenant Patrick. How are you feeling?"

Dennis frowned, gesturing to his bandaged arm. "I've been better."

Patrick smiled and lowered both hands to his sides. He leaned outward slightly from the desk as he spoke. "I understand you're retired LAPD."

"That's right. I made detective, but I put in my paperwork about six months ago."

Patrick had both a few pounds and a few years on Dennis, but less hair. He smiled again. "So, what brings you to our little patch of the desert?"

Dennis maintained a relaxed expression. Momentarily separating himself from the evening's events, he found himself mildly amused to be on the receiving end of the questions. He also knew that Patrick had already put these same questions to Tania Cooper in another room. Still, Dennis was an ex-cop, which he hoped would buy him some leeway, even in Bakersfield.

"I'm looking into a kidnap case," Dennis replied. "My daughter Ellie was abducted and we were damn lucky to get her back. Eventually, I decided to do something more meaningful." Answering Patrick's next question before he could ask it, he added, "Staying on the force wouldn't have given me the flexibility to pick my own cases." He finished with a grin, "And I was damn tired of paperwork."

"Amen to that." Patrick leaned back and folded his arms across his chest. "So you're working on the Keyes case. Find anything interesting?"

"Not yet. But I'd say someone taking a shot at me might be a new lead."

"That's a safe bet," Patrick chuckled. He had his own bemused look as he studied Mayer. He had a sharpness about him, and Patrick had a feeling he wasn't going to get the whole story out of the man.

"So who's the shooter?" Dennis asked.

"Don't know, yet. He's not talking and he didn't have any ID on him. We're running his prints now. I was hoping you might have some idea."

"Sorry. I wish I did."

Patrick pursed his lips, as if thinking. "Mind telling me again what happened?"

Dennis knew Patrick was asking to see how much his version varied from Tania's. "I was just leaving the house when this guy ran up out of the dark and took a couple shots at me. He grazed me, but it was too dark to fire back."

He left it at that. One thing cops knew was the less you said, the better. Especially if you were on the other side of the table.

"And what about the collision with your truck?"

Dennis shrugged. "Apparently Tania saw it all happen and drove into the bastard before he got away."

"That was awfully quick thinking. She must have kept the car running."

There were small holes in the story and Patrick had obviously noticed them. "I'm not sure if she kept the engine running or not."

"I see." Patrick feigned another thoughtful pause. "Why did Ms. Cooper stay in the truck? Why not go inside with you?"

"Katie Keyes' mother is in a pretty fragile emotional state. I didn't want her to feel overwhelmed." Dennis maintained his calm expression. It was a thin explanation, very thin. But not one easily disproven. Inconsistencies in someone's actions were easy to identify. It was much harder with a person's thoughts.

"I see. And what kinds of things did you talk to Ms. Keyes about?"

"I just went over the basics really. The day her daughter disappeared, any phone calls, that sort of

96

thing."

"And how many times had you been to the house?"

Damn it. Patrick knew about his earlier visit, which meant he talked to Anne Keyes. Worse, it meant that Keyes had talked to him. Did he know about Evan? If he did, it was going to be a long night.

"I visited her this morning too."

Patrick displayed a confused expression. "If you talked to her about the basics this evening, what did you talk about in the morning?"

"Pretty much the same stuff. Sometimes asking the same questions can jog a person's memory."

"And did it?"

Dennis shook his head. "Not this time."

"Hmm." Patrick nodded again and glanced at his watch. He decided they both had better things to do than play this cat and mouse game. Mayer was, after all, the victim here. Was Mayer trying to intentionally deceive him or was it just a result of being a cop for twenty years? Frankly, it didn't matter to him all that much. They had the shooter and that was who Patrick and his officers needed to spend their energy on. In the end, Mayer was trying to do a good thing, which was to find missing kids. And he wasn't about to get in the way of that. Who cared if he was trying to be secretive about it? Most officers didn't broadcast their occupations anyway.

"Okay, listen," Patrick said. "I'd like you to make sure you're available for more questioning later."

"No problem."

Patrick reached out his hand. Dennis stood and shook it.

"We pried your truck off the car and had it towed

here. Doesn't look too bad. You'll need some body work, but it's drivable."

"Thanks, Lieutenant."

"Sure thing. If you wait outside, I'll go get Ms. Cooper for you."

"Great."

"Incidentally, how do you know Ms. Cooper?"

Dennis didn't bat an eye. Patrick already knew the answer. "She works for my wife."

Patrick smiled one last time. "You need us to leave her name off the report? For your sake?"

Dennis laughed. "Nah. My wife knows she's with me."

The lieutenant opened the door for Mayer and followed him through, out into the open area. It was getting late and he needed to get to their friend who still wasn't talking. He decided not to bother asking Mayer his remaining questions. For example, why was Cooper sitting in the driver's seat when it was adjusted for someone much taller than she was? Perhaps someone even taller than Mayer.

A few minutes later, Dennis spotted Tania emerging from another office. She approached with a weary expression. "Can we go?"

"Yep."

Together they passed a row of empty desks and rounded the corner. At the end of a short hallway, they pushed the heavy automatic door open and crossed the marble-tiled lobby. Once outside, they were hit with the chill of the evening.

"So, do you know who it was that shot at you?" Tania asked in a low voice.

"I'll find out. But right now, we need to get out of here."

They approached Dennis' truck, parked in one of the nearby spots. The left front corner was smashed, but the right side had escaped with only some deep scrapes. It was when he noticed someone standing next to the truck that Dennis stopped. He studied the person for a moment before slowly continuing toward her.

"Hello, Mr. Mayer," said Anne Keyes.

"Are you alright?" Dennis asked.

"I was about to ask you that," she said sheepishly. "I think I owe you an apology. I guess you're for real after all."

Dennis introduced Tania, and Keyes nodded politely at her. "Am I going to have to forget you too?"

"Probably."

Keyes stepped forward. "I talked to the police. I had to. I figured it would seem strange if I didn't. But I didn't tell them about the young man you were with. I swear."

"I believe you."

She took a deep breath and exhaled. It was easily visible under the light from an overhead lamp post. "I'm sorry. For everything." She tried to blink the tears away. "I was afraid. Afraid to get excited again. Every new piece of information has given me a glimmer of hope only to be snuffed out again. I was afraid that maybe…"

"That maybe we were quacks?"

She couldn't even smile at his humor. Instead, she shook her head. "Please, Mr. Mayer. My Katie is all that matters to me. Without her, there is no reason for me to be here." Tears flowed down her cheeks. "Please find her!"

Mayer frowned and reached out for her. He pulled her in close as she sobbed into his chest. He knew what it felt like. A pain so deep that you couldn't even bear the memories. And a level of despair that led to the most terrible thoughts.

He wrapped his arms around Anne and held her. He knew it wasn't just about saving Katie Keyes anymore. It was about saving her mother too.

18

Shannon knew something was wrong. Dan Taylor hadn't spoken since leaving Bakersfield. Instead, he sat motionlessly in the seat next to her, staring out the window. She knew he needed to cool off, but when they got home and helped Evan inside, Taylor immediately disappeared upstairs.

When she reached his door, he was packing.

"You're leaving?"

"Yes." He kept his eyes down and continued packing.

"May I ask why?"

"Because Evan's going to get you all killed!" he growled.

"He's just trying to help."

Taylor opened his mouth angrily but stopped when he raised his eyes to find Evan standing next to Shannon. He pressed his lips together in frustration and then tried it again. "Sorry, kid. But you have no idea who you're dealing with. You'd better understand that tonight was a wake-up call for you." He glanced at Shannon. "For all of you."

"This isn't about Evan, or us. It's about you. You're afraid that if they find Evan, they'll find you too."

He stopped and straightened. "You're goddamn right. Three months. THREE MONTHS! That's all it took to find him! Did you really think no one would notice?!" Taylor looked at Evan. "You better hope that guy in Bakersfield is a nobody. And that you can stop this without anyone else finding out. That it's not too late. Because no matter how good your intentions are, more people are going to figure it out." He continued stuffing his clothes into his bag. "I *told* you swearing people to secrecy wasn't going to make a damn bit of difference." He finished with his things and zipped the bag closed. "Go ahead, kid. Be your own man. But when they find you, they're sure as hell not going to find me. Not here."

Taylor headed for the door and Evan abruptly backed up. Shannon stepped in front of him.

"Wait," she pleaded. "Just…wait."

"For what?"

"Please. My husband and Tania are still out there, and God only knows where. Please wait until I can at least be sure they're safe."

Taylor's brown eyes stared at her for a long time. "Fine," he said. "But when they get here, I'm done."

19

It was just after 2:15 a.m. when Dennis and Tania opened the front door of the house and walked in, exhausted. They were not surprised to see everyone on their feet and waiting for them. Everyone except Dan Taylor.

Even without the terrible night they'd had, Dennis knew something was wrong from the tone of Shannon's voice on the phone. Now in the living room, she silently eyed the bandaging on his arm and approached, wrapping her arms around him.

"Are you okay?"

Dennis hugged her tight and gave a tired smile. "It could have been a lot worse."

She pressed her head into his chest. "Thank God. I was so worried."

Tania watched briefly before turning to Evan, who was standing several feet away. She walked to him and smiled. "Hey, stranger."

Evan was clearly happy to see her. He began to reply but was stopped when she abruptly reached out and hugged him.

"Are *you* alright?"

Evan blinked. His head was suddenly spinning, for all the right reasons. "Yeah. I'm just tired."

Dennis gently released Shannon and looked past her shoulder to Mary, who stood back observing them all with a wide grin. His eyes then searched the room.

"Where's Taylor?"

His question was answered when heavy steps could be heard from the top of the stairs. A few moments later, two large feet appeared and descended. When he reached the bottom, Dennis spied the large bag gripped in Taylor's left hand.

"He's leaving," Shannon whispered.

If Dennis was surprised, he didn't show it. Taylor had been reluctantly cooperative at best since Evan told them what he intended to do.

He nodded at Taylor. "I'm glad you were there tonight."

Taylor squinted at Dennis. "Do you believe me now? Do you believe me when I tell you how dangerous this is?"

"I do."

Taylor motioned to Evan. "Then you'd better talk some sense into the boy before someone doesn't come home from one of your 'rescue missions.'"

Dennis and Evan exchanged glances but neither said a word.

"Do you even know who shot at you?" Taylor questioned.

Dennis turned back to him. "Yes. A local. He works as a bus driver."

"And did they tell you he's from Los Angeles?"

Dennis reacted with surprise. "Yes. How did you know that?"

Without taking his eyes off the man, Taylor reached into his pocket and pulled something out. He tossed the item onto a nearby coffee table. It was a wallet.

"I took it after I punched the son of a bitch out. Do you get it now? Do you understand? This guy isn't from Bakersfield, he's from here. Which means he followed you up there. In fact, he's probably been following you for a while." Taylor gave Evan a snide glance. "Did you *see* that?"

"No."

"No, you didn't," Taylor said. "You can see a lot of things, and you've only scratched the surface, but you'll never see who's coming for you. Do you hear me, boy? Unless you know who it is, you'll *never* see them coming until it's too late. That's what I've been trying to tell you. Every time you help someone, you provide another door for someone else to find you. This guy was a damn bus driver and he found you! Who will it be next?"

The room grew deathly quiet. Finally, Taylor sighed. "Look, you want to help people. I get it. But is it worth dying for?"

Evan stared at him, considering the question. His answer surprised everyone. "Yes."

Taylor flew into a rage. "Jesus Christ! Stop being so naïve. Death is if you're lucky! Has it even occurred to you that when someone finds you they're going to want to keep you *alive*?! How many people do you think are gonna be hurt when someone captures you and *uses* you like a weapon?!"

Evan swallowed hard. "I won't let them."

"Oh really?" Taylor smirked.

"Really."

When Evan didn't look away, Taylor grew quiet, staring at him eye to eye. He was the only one in the room who understood what Evan meant.

"Son," he said, with a tone of resignation. "You don't know what I know. You don't know what lengths people will go to get what you have. And trust me, they're heartless and damn creative." After a long silence, Taylor slung his bag over a shoulder and headed for the front door. "I can't warn you any better than that."

When he opened the door, Evan called out behind him.

"Mr. Taylor."

Wearily, Taylor turned around.

"Thank you."

With one last shake of his head, he was gone.

The room was quiet again. All five of them silent, still staring at the door.

Dennis spied the wallet on the coffee table and crossed the room to pick it up. He flipped through the leather fold, studying what few contents were inside.

Darias Black.

He was surprised to find that their attacker kept an ID in his wallet. But then again, he probably had to. If he ran into problems during the escape and had to rely on another form of travel, a photo ID might be necessary. Black must have felt that the risk of losing his ID was less than needing it and not having one. Unfortunately for him.

Dennis checked the larger pocket. It was filled with fifty-dollar bills. He sat down on the small couch and leaned back into the soft leather. "Well, this has been a crappy day."

Shannon grinned sympathetically and joined him on the couch. One by one, the other three crossed the room and sat down.

"So who do you think he is?" asked Mary.

"I don't know." Dennis flipped the wallet over, examining the worn leather. "My guess is someone with secrets. Secrets that Evan and I weren't supposed to find."

"But how could he have found Evan?"

"I've been thinking about that the whole way home. Up to this point we've been very careful. No pictures, no depositions, no mention of Evan at all. Not even by one of the families." He stared at the floor, thinking. "But we obviously missed something."

"Oh my God!" exclaimed Mary. "What if that guy Black is involved with the girl you're looking for?"

"It's possible. But I doubt it. Not living this far away."

"Why not? The guy sounded pretty careful to me. After all, if they were going to kidnap someone, wouldn't a smart person do it somewhere else?"

"Perhaps. But most kidnappers are related to the person kidnapped, and those who aren't don't usually stray very far. Generally speaking, they prefer the familiarity of their own environment. Being in a place you're not familiar with introduces all kinds of possibilities for mistakes."

"Well, maybe he wasn't the actual kidnapper," Shannon offered. "Maybe he was involved some other way."

"Maybe," Dennis nodded. "That would give him a reason to make sure we didn't continue. What do you think, Evan?"

He shrugged. "If there's a connection, it might help us."

"You would need something of his." He tossed the wallet back onto the small table. "Would a wallet work?"

"Probably."

"Waaait a minute," Shannon said, leaning quickly forward. "Not tonight."

"Not tonight, what?"

Evan's not doing anything more now. Not tonight. He's exhausted and we're not taking any chances. He's doing nothing but getting sleep."

"I didn't say tonight." Dennis frowned sarcastically. "But fine."

Dennis was the first one up. With the pain in his arm, he couldn't sleep. Even though it was technically only a graze, it felt serious enough that he knew a hospital visit was in his future. He popped two extra-strength Tylenols and took a sip of coffee. He hated taking pills but they did take the edge off, keeping the pain tolerable.

He sat down quietly at the small kitchen table and watched the rising sun peek over the dark green southern magnolia trees in his backyard. The events of the previous night happened so fast that they felt surreal. He was thankful Evan hadn't been struck. They were both exceptionally lucky he tripped just before the shots.

Dennis heard steps behind him and turned around to find Evan entering the kitchen. He joined Dennis at the table and reached into one of his pajama pockets. Evan then quietly laid Darias Black's wallet on the table in front of him.

"He's not involved."

"With Katie Keyes?"

Evan shook his head.

Dennis nodded to the wallet. "You're not supposed to do that alone."

"It was quick."

"Hmm." Dennis picked up the wallet and turned it over. "So, no link to Katie Keyes at all?"

There was no answer.

Dennis looked at Evan, who was sitting still, staring down at the kitchen table. He cocked his head. "Evan?"

Still nothing.

Dennis reached out. "Evan, are you alright?"

Finally, he blinked and looked up. His face seemed pale. "What?"

"What is it?"

He stared at Dennis for a moment before dropping his gaze back down. "It's that man."

Dennis held the wallet up. "This guy?"

"He didn't take Katie. But he did other things. A lot of 'em."

"Bad things."

Evan nodded.

"Other kids?"

Evan nodded again.

Dennis leaned back in his chair. *That's why Black was afraid of him and Evan. Sooner or later, they might look at his case. And find out what he had done.*

Dennis grew angry. It happened every time. Sick criminals never had a problem dealing out pain and suffering to others. But when justice came due, every single one of them turned and ran. Not only were they sick, but their cowardice knew no bounds. At that moment, he would have given anything to be locked alone in a room with Black. For some men, death was the only rehabilitation.

He observed the blank stare on Evan's face. "Are you going to be okay?"

Evan painfully shook his head from side to side. "It's too late for them."

Dennis raised his hand and put it gently on Evan's

back. He had no words.

21

The hamburger joint was less than two blocks from Glendale's Memorial Hospital and just off Cerritos Avenue. Evan took another bite of his hamburger and peered down the street at a small section of the famous Forest Lawn cemetery.

"Remember, you're going to call me twice a day."

He turned again to his mother, sitting across the table from him. "I remember."

Mary returned to the table with a cup of water and sipped it. "Shannon called. They should be here in a few minutes." She looked at Evan. "You have your phone, right?"

He rolled his eyes.

They were worried and he understood why. It was the furthest they had gone for a rescue mission. All the other children they found had been in the Los Angeles area.

Looking back toward the hospital, Evan spotted the Mayers approaching on foot in the distance. It looked like Mr. Mayer's left arm was in a sling.

With a few more bites, he polished off his burger and wiped his mouth. He quickly finished his shake, ending with a slurping sound through his straw. He was ready.

Mrs. Mayer's sister, Mary, had lent them her Subaru and made them both promise they would take care of it. When Evan stood up, a large commercial bus caught his eye as it passed outside along South

Brand Boulevard.

Evan thought of Dan Taylor and wondered where he was.

As train stations went, Los Angeles' Union Station, or LAUS, was still quite beautiful, even as it approached one hundred years old. The original ballot measure to build the station was controversial at the time, but in present day, it serviced a staggering 60,000 daily passengers.

At that moment, Dan Taylor stood in one of the station's large rooms, examining some of the building's original architecture from days gone by. His eyes followed the sharp lines of the interior marble walls and ended on the terra-cotta tiles.

He took a deep breath, noting the unique smell. Oddly, it somehow reminded him of both history and the future at the same. More than that, it brought out a strange feeling inside Taylor. A feeling of years having passed without him, a result of his seclusion. And to his surprise, a feeling of regret.

Standing quietly among the hundreds of bustling passengers, Taylor suddenly got a sensation that he was being watched. He looked from side to side and seeing no one, he slowly turned and scanned the area behind him. He stopped upon meeting a pair of young eyes.

It was a boy, staring at him with the familiar eyes of a Down syndrome child. The boy was staring at Taylor with a giant grin on his face, seemingly unaware of the crowd around him.

Taylor followed his line of sight and turned back

around, trying to determine if the boy was, in fact, looking at him. He was. He was sitting next to his mother, waving excitedly at Taylor as if he'd spotted a friend.

Dan Taylor stared back for a long time. Finally, his frown softened and he waved back. He began to turn and head for his train's platform when he stopped. On the wall above the young boy's head, something caught his eye. It was a large picture. An advertisement.

The ad was a large public service announcement, featuring the faces of five young children, with ages ranging from what looked to be about eight years old to probably eleven, who had disappeared or been abducted in the last few years. Taylor stood there, transfixed on the middle picture of another young boy. His reddish blonde hair was slightly tussled with light freckles covering his nose and cheeks.

It was a face Taylor had seen before when he glimpsed Black's wallet.

He could not move. Taylor stared, paralyzed at seeing the young face, frozen in time by someone's camera lens. The boy's eyes were full of life and innocence. He wondered where the child was when the picture was taken.

But what truly devastated Taylor was wondering where *he himself* was when the boy's picture was taken.

He was hiding in the mountains, that's where. Unexpectedly, Taylor felt flushes of emotion wash over him. The first was sadness at the terrifying panic the boy must have experienced when he was abducted. The second was anger. Who were these sick people that preyed on children? His last wave of emotion was that of shame.

114

22

It took less than thirty minutes for the taxi cab to find the address. When it did, the driver stopped in front of the nondescript corner house. Taylor paid the fare and stepped out onto the hot asphalt. Without a word, he pulled his bag out from behind him and slung it over his shoulder. The taxi promptly drove off, leaving him staring from the street.

He'd remembered the address from the wallet. It was Black's home. Painted a faded green, with bushes and a small hedge, the house was in desperate need of maintenance. Just above them were two dirty window screens.

The old street was quiet. Most people were indoors, trying to avoid the unrelenting midday heat. Once the taxi had made its right turn, Taylor looked back at the house and followed the sidewalk around the corner, toward the tall wooden fence. He casually made his way along the fence until he reached the end corner, and then circled around the back of the yard.

The fence post was easy to climb and he hit the ground inside with a thud. He listened carefully. The only noise was coming from a neighbor's window. He walked lightly down one side of the backyard toward the house. Unlike the weed-covered ground, the rear screened-in porch was neat and organized with a small table, various tools, and cleaning supplies stacked in the corner.

Taylor listened again. Still nothing. He snaked a

finger through the worn, screen door handle and pulled. It didn't open. He peered in from the side and spotted the latch which secured the screen using an eye bolt on the other side. It wasn't strong. Just something to keep the door closed. Taylor wrapped four thick fingers through the handle and looked around one more time. With a sudden and forceful jerk, one of the brackets splintered from the wooden frame and the door fell outward, partly open. The noise was louder than Taylor had hoped and he quickly stepped inside.

He scanned the porch, including the table and the tools. There was no police tape, no footmarks on the floorboards, nothing that indicated the cops had arrived yet. It was just a matter of time. No doubt they were in the process of getting a warrant.

Taylor knew time was short. He assessed the door to the house, painted the same dull green with two deadbolts above the knob. He didn't expect the door to be unlocked and he was right. Getting through the door would be nearly impossible, so for the sake of expediency, he grabbed an old spade from the group of tools. Taylor then broke a smaller pane of what appeared to be the kitchen window.

He immediately ran the tool around the edges of the frame, clearing the glass, and was inside before anyone had time to peek over the fence. And with any luck, Black's neighbors didn't like him enough to take much notice of an intruder: a distinct possibility.

Inside, the house was deathly quiet. He stood away from the window and examined the immaculate kitchen. It was spotless. Nothing was left out on the counter, and a subtle scent of pine was present from most likely a recent cleanser or disinfectant.

Taylor silently followed the hallway and peeked into the front room before scanning the front yard for any movement.

He had to hurry. He checked the rest of the house and returned to the kitchen. There, he pulled a white vinyl chair out and away from the table.

The chair squeaked momentarily when Taylor lowered his bulky frame into it. Taking a deep breath, he popped two pills into his mouth and chewed them, moving the remaining bits under his tongue. Reaching inside his shirt, Taylor pulled the chain over his neck and tightly gripped his metal cross in his palm.

He managed his breathing until his pulse began to slow. A moment later he dropped his chin and closed his eyes.

After glimpsing the house, Taylor was back in the hallway, intently examining the walls. The hanging portraits were of an older couple: most likely Darias Black's parents. Halfway down the hall, a tall but thin bookcase covered part of the left side. Its shelves were filled with old, used books and Taylor recognized several classic titles.

It wasn't the books that Taylor was searching. It was the dimensions of the bookcase itself. He stood back, studying it. Stepping closer, he examined the large brackets attaching the case to the wall. Both were firmly secured. He stepped to the other side and ran his fingers over the second set of brackets. This time they moved. He felt for resistance and found they both slid down nearly an inch. With a heave, he pushed the side of the bookcase, causing it to slide sideways and revealing what he was looking for: a dark, narrow doorway.

Taylor leaned his head into the opening, searching for a light switch. He soon found it and flipped it on, bathing the small room in light.

From the inside, he could now see it was actually a third bedroom in the house. It was smaller and the door had evidently been removed, replaced with the bookcase instead.

He turned around and scanned the room. The walls were completely covered in pictures. Pictures of children from various angles and distances. Some were taken of children getting off a bus. Others at what appeared to be parks or swimming pools.

The grotesque *wallpaper* was bad enough, but it was the small closet that turned Taylor's stomach. The doors to the closet had been removed and inside was what he could only assume was a shrine of some kind. Items adorned each side. In the middle sat a table beneath several close-up pictures. All of the close-ups were children, one of whom Taylor recognized immediately. He'd seen his face on the wall of the train station. The same young boy.

Taylor put a hand on the wall to steady himself. The feelings of fear and sickness in the room were overwhelming. Suddenly, a realization hit him that nearly caused him to vomit. The items hanging on each side of the closet rod were articles of their clothing. Trophies.

He whirled around at the wallpaper again and the nauseousness instantly compounded. He was stumbling toward the door when his eye caught something in one of the pictures. The photo had been taken at a park and a shadow could be seen on the ground in the picture. No doubt the shadow of Darias Black, standing on a sidewalk while he snapped the photo. But it wasn't Black's shadow that caught Taylor's eye. It was part of a second shadow, standing next to the first.

The revelation hit Taylor like a two-by-four. He raced to the small opening and squeezed back through. He spun to his left and stared back down the hall. There were four doors, two lining each side. As he ran down the hallway, he could see one was a bathroom and the second a small closet. The other two were bedrooms. *Two bedrooms. And both were used.*

Someone else lived in the house with Black!

23

Lars Black was growing nervous. His brother was still in custody in Bakersfield, and there was very little time left before a more thorough investigation began. Their lawyer confirmed that since no fingerprints were found on the gun ditched at the scene, the case was largely going to rest on the eyewitness account of Dennis Mayer. Which meant Lars needed to make sure Mayer would not be able to testify. And he needed to do it fast.

The problem was that he couldn't find Mayer. He'd reached his house that morning only to find the place empty. There was, however, another way. Lars discovered that Dennis Mayer's wife was a psychiatrist in Glendale. Her office was easy to locate and he waited for her to show up, which she did later that afternoon. But her stop was brief. She and her young daughter left minutes after arriving and drove across town to someone else's home. They had been there ever since.

So had Lars. The younger Black was now calmly watching the house and, more than anything, waiting for the sun to go down.

"They're going to be fine." Mary reassured her sister, placing a fresh cup of coffee down in front of her. Down the hall, her kids could be heard playing with their cousin Ellie.

"I know."

Mary stared at her sister. She knew that look on her face. "But?" she added.

Shannon frowned. "But…I don't know how long I can do this for."

"What do you mean?"

"I mean things are different now. At first it was just search and rescue. I didn't," she paused, "…I didn't expect it to get like this. I really thought Taylor was overreacting. I didn't expect them to actually become *targets*."

Mary took a sip from her own mug. "Neither did I."

"This has become dangerous, Mary. And I'm not convinced Evan's health problems are behind him yet. I'm worried they're just morphing into something else. Maybe something deeper."

Mary stared at her sister for a long moment. "Well, since you brought it up…I asked you to come over because there's something else I wanted to talk to you about. About Evan."

Shannon raised her eyebrows expectantly.

"I was thinking about what Evan and Dennis said, about the attack last night. Did anything stand out to you about the timing of it all?"

"Not really. Why?"

"Well, I've been thinking of something Evan said. About the gunshots. And the timing."

Shannon stared pensively. "You mean when he fell?"

"Exactly. Evan said something actually caused him to lose his balance."

"Right. He said it was a seizure, which is why I'm

worried that his problems, or at least his symptoms, may be changing into something else."

"It's possible," Mary nodded, pursing her lips. "But there may be another explanation."

"Such as?"

"At one point Evan made a comment that there was some kind of flash that accompanied what he thought was a seizure."

"Right. But a lot of things can happen during seizures. Mental disorientation, for example."

"Yes, I know," Mary agreed. "But what if that's not what it was? What if it wasn't disorientation at all?"

Shannon's expression grew curious.

Mary continued. "He said it was a *flash*. Does that sound like disorientation to you?"

Shannon brushed away a strand of short brown hair. "Well, disorientations can be…" Her words slowed to a crawl and she stopped, thinking.

Mary went on. "Remember, Dennis was the one who described the gunshots. Evan was already on the ground, right?"

"More or less."

"But…when Dennis mentioned the shots, he said there were two flashes."

"Right."

"And Dennis hadn't seen Evan until they were both back here."

"I'm not following."

Mary fixed her eyes on Shannon. "What I'm saying is that Dennis told us the shots occurred *after* Evan had tripped. And Evan said he saw a flash and tripped, *before* the shots. It's been bugging me ever since I heard it. I think they were too excited to catch that detail."

"Maybe things just happened too fast."

"Maybe. But they both remembered it clearly. What if they're both correct?" Mary leaned forward onto her small dining room table. "Shannon, what if they both saw the *same flash*?"

Shannon furrowed her brow. "What do you mean, the same flash?"

"What I mean is, what if Evan actually saw the flash a split second *before* it happened?!"

Lars Black eased the back door closed behind him. It was dark inside the garage with little of the day's remaining light creeping in through the cracks. He crossed through the darkness and approached the inside door to the house, where he paused to pull a thin cloth mask over his head.

He put his hand on the doorknob and turned it gently. It was unlocked. He began pushing the door open very slowly. Slow enough to allow him to stop immediately at the slightest sound.

As the crack between the door and jam grew bigger, Black could hear both women talking. They sounded close-by. From the opposite direction, he could make out the sounds of children down a hallway. He spotted a picture on the wall and could see a woman's head reflecting in the clear glass. She was just around the corner with her back to the hallway. And the second woman sounded just as close.

Both women turned when they heard the door creak. But it was too late. Lars Black leaped into the carpeted hall and rounded the corner before either of them could react. They gasped and froze when he pressed a gun against the side of Shannon's head.

"Where is he?" Black whispered.

Both women were still in shock.

"Where is he?!" Black repeated, raising his voice.

Shannon dared not move. She remained erect in her chair without moving a muscle. "W…who?"

Black hissed through his mask. "Your husband!"

Oh my God! Shannon fought to keep calm. "I…I don't know. Driving maybe."

"Driving *where*?!"

Shannon didn't answer. She struggled to even think. "I'm not sure."

"Then call him."

Shannon stared at her sister. She blinked, trying to remember where her phone was. "Uh…" Suddenly, her eyes grew wider than her sister's. *Ellie had her phone.* Shannon had let her play games on it on the way over. She still had it. "I…I don't have my phone," she said calmly. "I think I left it in the car."

Black scanned the room and spotted the kitchen phone near the wall. He nodded to Mary. "Get that one!"

Mary scrambled from the table and practically lunged at it. She grabbed the cordless handset and turned back toward Black at the table.

Shannon was petrified. Her mind raced, trying to think of what to do. She managed to look up into the eyes of her sister only to find her standing still, fixated on Black. Shannon nearly screamed. *Give him the damn phone!*

What Shannon didn't notice was the slight shift in her sister's eyes.

A loud *thunk* came from behind Shannon. The gun fell from her temple and she felt Black's body waver. She jumped as her attacker crumpled abruptly to the floor. Confused, she looked at her sister and then spun in her chair.

She was speechless to find Dan Taylor standing behind her, holding a giant wrench. Without a word, he peered down at Black's motionless body. He stepped closer and reached down, pulling the cloth mask off. Black's dark-haired head fell back to the floor with a thump.

Taylor turned to Mary when he heard the kids laugh in the other room. "Don't let them come out here!"

Without a word, Mary bolted down the hallway.

Shannon stood up and pushed away from the table. She was surprised once again as Tania came running in behind Taylor with a golf club in her hand.

"You can be one goddamn hard woman to find," growled Taylor.

"I'm sorry," Tania breathed heavily. "I didn't have Mary's number on my phone. But I remembered where she lived."

Mary reemerged from the hall just as Shannon took another step back, staring down at Black. "Who is he?"

"The brother of the man who shot at your husband last night."

"Is he dead?"

"I doubt it. But you're safe now." Taylor looked around. "Where's Evan?"

Mary folded her arms. "They left already."

Taylor shook his head in frustration. "Christ, when is someone going to listen to me? When are you all going to help me talk Evan out of this? What he's doing is dangerous! And this is only the beginning. This is not something that he should be playing games with just to be a hero."

"He's not."

Taylor turned around and looked at Tania. "What?"

"I said he's not!"

"He's not what?"

Her face grew angry. "He's not trying to be a hero!"

"Yeah? Well then, what do you call it?"

Shannon watched the young woman clench her fists and take a small step toward Taylor.

"Have you ever bothered to ask him? Ask him why he's doing this? No. Of course not. It's easier for you just to judge, isn't it?!" Tania slowly shook her head. "If you had, you would know why. You would know why, and you would see that he's not trying to be anything. Especially not a hero!"

Taylor squinted at her. "What are you talking about?"

"Have you ever asked him anything at all? Like where he grew up or what his childhood was like?"

Taylor didn't answer.

"I didn't think so. Maybe you should start by asking where his father is. Have you ever thought about that?"

Again, no answer.

"His father is dead. He died when Evan was six." Tania glared at Taylor. "Do you want to know how? In a fire! Their house caught fire and Evan's father

126

saved him. He saved Evan and tried to save his four-year-old sister too. But he couldn't find her. He went back in and died trying to find his daughter."

All three stared at Tania in stunned silence.

"Those are the two pictures that Evan keeps in the locket he carries with him. He blames himself for their deaths. Especially his sister's. He thinks that if his father hadn't gotten him out first, he would have gotten his sister out instead. In other words, he thinks his sister is dead because of *him*."

Taylor looked down at Tania with a pained expression. "I didn't know that."

"Don't you see? Evan's not doing this to be a hero. He's doing it as a way to find forgiveness. Forgiveness from his sister, for something that was never his fault in the first place. It's guilt that's driving him. Not some dream of being a hero."

Shannon's eyes began to well. "My God. It all makes sense now," she said, wiping a tear away. She looked at the others. "Evan's not just trying to save these children. Deep down he's trying to save his *sister*."

"And that's why he won't stop," added Tania. "Because he can't."

Taylor stared at her in silence, unblinking. After a long moment, he sighed and sat down in one of the chairs.

24

Evan startled himself awake. He looked around from the passenger seat of the car and slowly relaxed.

"You okay?"

He peered at Mr. Mayer sitting behind the wheel and nodded. "Just a bad dream."

"Are you sure you're up for this, Evan?"

"Yeah."

Dennis Mayer gave him a sidelong glance. He wasn't so sure. Evan was much quieter than normal. The attack in Bakersfield had obviously shaken him. Dennis turned his attention back to the long stretch of road ahead of them with the desert on either side extending as far as the eye could see. He wondered if this might be their last rescue mission together.

After several minutes, Dennis tilted his head. "So do we know exactly where we're going yet?"

"I think so. I'm pretty sure the tunnels are east of the city."

Dennis frowned, thoughtfully. "I hope we can find them. Vegas is a big city."

"So are the tunnels," replied Evan.

The project began in 1986 when Las Vegas became desperate to address one of the city's most dangerous problems, a problem virtually unknown to most tourists. But for those having been caught in a sudden flash flood, they were well aware that the experience could be absolutely terrifying.

Las Vegas was situated on the floor of the Mojave Desert, running along Nevada's southern region. Its floor became notoriously deadly when the valley's parched sands fell victim to unexpected heavy thunderstorms. Aided by mountains on all sides, some flash floods produced walls of water that were over forty feet high and utterly devastating.

The answer was as big as the problem itself: more than two hundred miles of concrete flood tunnels. The tunnels took decades to build and now stretched in virtually every direction deep beneath the glowing lights of downtown Las Vegas, the Entertainment Capital of the World.

Yet these enormous tunnels, the largest civil engineering advancement in the history of the city, didn't take long to become one of Vegas' darkest secrets. It was a strange irony given the metropolis's worldwide reputation and title of *Sin City*. A title the giant flood tunnels of Las Vegas had only reinforced.

The secret was that the enormous labyrinth became something altogether different to the city's downtrodden. The tunnels were used as *housing* for thousands of the city's destitute, poor, and criminal elements.

Miles of graffiti covered the dirty, concrete walls and intermittent rays of light left the flood tunnels resembling a post-apocalyptic world. Trash and rubble covered much of the ground and, in the main corridors, streams of polluted water trickled past, bound for an unseen outlet.

But within those dark, cold corridors were the people. Living amongst the rats and scorpions were the gray and unkempt faces of souls whom civilization had forgotten or rejected. Most sat on scavenged pieces of foam or cloth, staring into the dark bleakness of a day-by-day existence. An ambitious few managed to set up makeshift tables or perhaps a bookshelf, stocked with old, discarded books.

But it was the sounds that were the worst. For miles, moans and screams echoed ominously through perfectly conductive, four-foot thick walls.

With most police unwilling to enter, there was no safety and no protection. The dank halls resembled modern day catacombs, symbolizing in many ways a very last gasp of humanity.

The other girls were still sleeping. Twelve-year-old Katie Keyes could hear them breathing nearby in the darkness. Her nose had long since adjusted to the musky, almost rotten, smell of the damp concrete around her. Her ears had become even more sensitive. She could hear every sound around her, including the echoes far down the bowels of the other tunnels. From a great distance, the scurrying of people sounded almost identical to the rats moving around her.

At first she had been frightened by the rats constantly moving in and out of their things, even over their cardboard beds. But over time, their presence became almost comforting.

She had been there for almost a month, and the other two girls had been there even longer. Aside from a brief visit every day by one of their captors, the three were all each other had; all they had to try to make sense out of what had happened to them and how they got there. The other two were younger than Katie, both eleven years old. The youngest, Deena, barely talked anymore.

All three girls were from California and Deena was from Bakersfield, like Katie. Brooke was from a small town outside Los Angeles.

None of them really knew what exactly happened, but they all remembered being taken in the same way. A car stopping to ask directions and then a gun pointed at them, telling them to get into the car. Something they no longer talked about. They initially tried to talk about other things. Good things. But now they were sinking. Sinking into an utterly hopeless and fearful existence.

Katie didn't know what time it was. None of them did. Sometimes it was light outside when the men showed up with food.

Now she was awake. Awoken by a strange dream. It was not like her other dreams of home, which always ended in tears when she woke in the darkness to realize where she really was. This one was different. Instead of seeing her school or her family, she saw something else. A face. A boy's face, not too much older than she was. Maybe in high school.

She couldn't see anything in the blackness, but she could feel her heart still racing. She groped around for her thin blanket and pulled it around her shoulders, trying to decide whether she should tell the other girls. After all, it was just a dream and down here it was hard for them to have hope. But the boy's face seemed so real. And it was what he said that caused her to suddenly wake up. He said something about *heaven*…and that he was coming.

25

Amara Seng sat inside the dark interior of his Mercedes Benz S550. He watched silently, from the Northeast corner of the Excalibur Hotel, as dozens of people crossed over the West Tropicana Avenue causeway. His dark eyes darted absently from person to person as he listened to the ringing on the phone.

With darker than average skin, a wide nose, and short, straight black hair, his Asian features were unmistakable. And while he could pass for American born, it was his strong accent that gave away his status as a relatively recent immigrant. He had been in the States for just over five years now, and what he lacked in naturalization, he made up for in ruthless ambition.

Seng had grown up in the streets of Phnom Penh, Cambodia, surviving on little more than his wits and a raw desire to live. By the age of eleven, he had seen it all. Virtually every dark side of humanity the mind could imagine. A world that shaped him into the very definition of a survivor. Seng endured by understanding the world around him for what it was: a world of desire and resources. No matter what it was, everything could be broken down into resources. Whether it was drugs, food, fuel, or a place to sleep, it was all about the *value* one could extract from any item. Any item, including human beings.

To Seng, it was easy. For one person to win, someone else had to lose. The world was not fair, and because of that, winners were simply the ones who did what needed to be done to ensure they didn't lose.

Seng glanced briefly at the phone just before the call was answered. Both phones were disposables, used to call only one number. And this was it.

"Susaday."

Seng grinned slightly with tight lips. It was a code of sorts to let him know the conversation was safe, but in all of his dealings with the man, Seng had never heard the word pronounced correctly. He scanned the dark parking lot around him. "Susaday."

"We ready?"

Seng nodded. "I bring them tonight."

"Perfect," the voice responded. "How many?"

"Two."

"See you in three hours."

The call ended and Seng glanced back at the console. Sixteen seconds. Not nearly long enough for a trace. Tonight he'd lose the phone on the freeway anyway.

He started the car again and gazed out over its black hood. *Trafficking* in Vegas was rampant, but it usually involved prostitutes or runaways. Anyone could do that. Enticing emotionally lost girls into a better life took almost no effort at all, especially when you didn't have to make good on your promises.

What Seng offered was something entirely different. Most traffickers dealt with whatever product they could get. But some buyers had better, more expensive taste. They didn't want girls strung out on drugs or booze. And that's what Seng provided: young, clean, and educated. Which meant a much higher price per head.

Seng's merchandise was also taken from richer

neighborhoods, which provided two big advantages. Kids in richer neighborhoods were typically clean and rarely had serious health problems. But more importantly, they were weak. Spoiled their whole lives, the well-off kids had no *fight* in them. Instead, they had become brainwashed with a sense of entitlement or self-worth, a life spent receiving everything they wanted simply by asking. Their will was the easiest to break.

However, Seng had a problem. He couldn't deliver all three tonight as planned. The last one wasn't coming around. While most broke easily after two weeks in pitch blackness, this older one wasn't. She was still resisting inside. Fighting. And Seng had a reputation to protect. He couldn't deliver something that wasn't going to cooperate. He'd seen it before. Every so often, there was a resister. One who either couldn't, or wouldn't, be broken in the limited amount of time that he had. The last thing he wanted to do was to hold on to these resisters too long. The longer he had them, the harder they made it, until something slipped. Until someone discovered Seng's operation, no matter how careful he was.

And Seng was careful. The other *sellers* in Vegas were sloppy. Damaged goods meant a certain type of seller. Never very sophisticated and usually as high as the product they were moving. Not Seng. He knew there were teams of law enforcement out there, searching for people just like him. Trafficking was too widespread to ever stop but that didn't mean the authorities would stop looking, or stop trying to end it.

It's why Seng kept his operation small. Just a few at a time. Hold them, break them, and move them.

It was a business.

In another year, Seng would move on to another city before anyone got too close. And his ruthless efficiency meant he had to do something about his current problem. The older girl had to go. Getting rid of resisters was not hard to do. Not in three thousand square miles of desert.

Katie lay quietly on her cardboard bed, listening to the two other girls breathe while they slept. She would wait a little longer.

The feeling was still there. The memory of her dream and her pounding heart, which hadn't slowed. She prayed that it was true. She didn't know how much longer she could go on. Her mind had already slipped into the bad place that the other girls were in, but she'd caught herself. She couldn't let herself go there again. If she did, she wasn't sure if she could get back out.

Poor Deena. Katie wasn't sure if she would ever come out. Every time their captors came to bring them food and remove the bucket, there was enough light for Katie to see the other girls' faces. Both were dirty and chalk white, but Brooke still had a look in her eyes, showing at least part of her was still there. But not Deena.

If Deena were still in there somewhere, maybe Katie's dream would help her. She hoped so.

Katie wondered how much longer she had. How much longer until she too gave up like the others? They may have given up sooner, but no one could last forever. However, Katie had something neither

Brooke nor Deena had. The image of her incredible father. His strong face and intense eyes that she would always remember.

She blinked in the darkness, suddenly trying to figure out exactly how long she had been here. It was getting harder. How many days? Her father had been gone for over two years. He died when she was ten.

A wave of anxiety washed over her. *Oh no. If she couldn't remember how long she'd been down here, she couldn't remember how long her father had been gone!*

Wait. How many times had the men come down with food? They came once a day. She had kept track in the beginning but eventually gave up. She remembered the number twenty, so that meant, like, a month? Maybe more.

Her anxiety eased and her thoughts slowly returned to her father. *Two and a half years. He'd only been gone for two and a half.*

He was so strong. He was retired from the Army. What was the word her mother always teased him with? *Intense.* He was intense. But he knew it and would even laugh about it sometimes when they both ganged up on him. He wasn't mean. He was just intense and strong. He never gave up on anything. Now, over two years later, any bad memories had faded, leaving only happy ones. She missed him so much. Her mother too, but deep down, even when she didn't like his rules, she had always been a daddy's girl. And it was he who she thought about most.

Katie heard Brooke stir on her own piece of cardboard. After waiting a few minutes, she finally called to her companion in a whispered voice.

"Brooke, are you awake?"

"Yes."

Katie scampered toward her in the darkness. "I have something to tell you."

Her heart was beating even faster now. She wasn't sure what it was, but something inside made her sure that she was right. *She was leaving tonight.*

It never occurred to Katie that it might be for a very different reason.

26

"Are you sure?"

Evan stood on the edge of an off-ramp from the 215 Freeway, staring out at the skyline of Las Vegas. Only a slight gleam of light could still be seen as the sun prepared for its final drop behind the barren mountains. The giant city and its brilliant lights were clearly visible in the distance.

"Yes."

Dennis Mayer followed Evan's gaze out across the valley toward the cityscape. "This is the right direction?"

Evan nodded. "This is what I saw. It's just ahead, I think." He pointed downhill. "Down there."

"Okay," Dennis shrugged. It all seemed rather uncertain to him. But why start doubting the kid now? Besides, even if they made a couple of missteps, they had some time. They were here now, and whether it was today or tomorrow or even the next day, Evan was sure she was here and alive. They just had to start looking.

"Let's go," he said, speaking over his shoulder while heading back to the car. He stopped by the door, waiting, until Evan finally turned and joined him.

"We have to hurry."

"Why? What is it?"

"I have a strange feeling that something is about to happen."

The opening was huge, like a giant gaping mouth emerging from under the earth. In the bright beams of their flashlights, it looked like a monster stretching its long neck to swallow them whole.

And it could. The entrance was at least eight feet wide by nearly five feet high. Garbage and debris lay around them, as if the monster had suddenly vomited at their feet. Two different broken shopping carts and dozens of tattered scraps of clothing all greeted them ominously, scattered among the rubble and graffiti as far into the mouth as they could see.

"Good God." Dennis stepped over a small mound of trash and peered deeper into the darkness. "In here?"

Evan nodded quietly. He was staring down the rectangular tube with more than trepidation. It was pure fear.

"You're really sure about this?"

"She's in there...somewhere."

Dennis stepped back carefully. He then climbed up the steep dirt embankment and peered over the top. They were still at least three miles from downtown. *How far did these things go?* With a shake of his head, he slid back down and returned to the entrance, where Evan was waiting.

"Do you know *where* inside?"

Evan closed his eyes. He tried to retrace what he had seen. "Mostly. But there are a lot of these tunnels, all in different directions. I didn't see the whole path, but I tried to remember what I could see." He shined the beam of his flashlight down the tunnel. It illuminated less than a hundred feet in.

"It's kind of complicated. Like a maze."

Dennis reached under his jacket and fingered his gun reassuringly. This was not a good idea. Anyone could be waiting inside these tunnels. Not to mention that once inside with their lights, Dennis and Evan would be visible to others long before they could see them. And anyone hiding in there sure as hell wasn't looking for friends.

"How far in is she?"

Evan shrugged. He wasn't very good with distances. "I don't know. Maybe a mile."

"A mile?!"

"Maybe less. I'm not exactly sure."

"Jesus," Dennis mumbled. He turned to Evan. "Okay, listen. You stay behind me. *Right* behind me! The whole time."

"Okay."

"If you can't reach out and touch me then you're too far away. Got it?"

"Got it."

Dennis felt for his gun again, this time subconsciously. He shined his light down the tunnel and took a deep breath. Stepping over the small trickle of blackish water, he entered the tunnel with Evan close behind.

They were less than twenty feet in before, outside, large raindrops began dotting the ground.

27

Seng watched the drops continue to cover his windshield after each pass of the wipers. He listened carefully to a radio newscast about the incoming storm. It was perfect timing. He'd been gambling against the weather for a couple weeks and won. He would have the girls out in plenty of time.

They just needed to hurry.

He slowed the Mercedes in front of a downtown parking garage, stopping just long enough for the passenger door to be pulled open. One of his partners, named Kou, slid in next to him. Before the door was even closed, Seng accelerated again and pulled back out into traffic.

Just south of the main "Strip," the Las Vegas Outlet Center was one of the larger shopping malls in the city. Housing over one hundred thirty stores, the Outlet Center covered an area greater than most Vegas casinos. More importantly, it had a much larger parking lot.

They needed a car and the mall was an ideal place to steal one. At maximum capacity, the parking lot could accommodate tens of thousands of vehicles, without the hundreds of video cameras to go with it. And during the holidays, most vehicle owners would be inside for hours.

Seng and Kou were situated on the edge of the busiest entrance to the lot, waiting. Watching for the right model. A Honda or Toyota preferably. Ideally, a late 1990's model. There was a reason they were the most common car stolen. The ignition systems were still easy to bypass, before the new era of modern deterrents like smart keys and tracking systems. On top of that, Hondas and Toyotas were some of the most affordable and desirable cars on the roads, which made them easy to find. More importantly, it made them less likely to stand out in the eyes of local law enforcement.

They needed a fresh vehicle for the *extraction*. One with a decent-sized trunk. Fortunately, young girls were still relatively small.

Once the extraction was over, they could be out of Vegas within fifteen minutes and over the Arizona border within an hour. After that, Kou would find another dark parking lot and remove a set of Arizona plates. The car would eventually be abandoned somewhere in New Mexico after delivery was made.

They noticed a green Toyota Camry drive past, headed toward the center lot. Seng shifted into drive and eased forward. They followed slowly, until the Camry turned, and then continued on to the next parking aisle. They watched the Toyota park while Seng did the same, keeping the car in view. A few moments later, the Camry's driver side door opened and a woman got out.

Seng and Kou waited for several minutes until the woman reached the double glass doors of the department store and disappeared inside. Without a word, Kou withdrew a long thin piece of metal from his jacket and pushed his door open. He stepped out into the now drizzling rain and gave Seng a brief nod.

He knew where to meet next.

28

Evan stumbled through the stream of water running down the middle of the tunnel and bumped into Dennis.

"You okay?"

"Yeah. Sorry." He was still weak and struggling in the darkness. The water was getting deeper, now above his ankles, making his footing slippery. He was trying hard to endure the smell of rotting garbage.

Another tattered mattress came into view, this time with two people sitting on it. It was covered by what appeared to be a few layers of dingy blankets with a man and woman sitting atop and leaning against the wall. They seemed almost unaware of the deepening water running along one of the edges of the mattress, soaking the bottom and half of the blankets.

Next to them were several blue plastic crates, layered with old planks of boards forming makeshift shelves. Several books were stacked on top, along with what looked to be an old camping lantern. Evan peered at them curiously as they sloshed past, wondering why the lantern was not lit.

Like many of the others, neither the woman nor the man bothered to look up at them.

A few minutes later, they reached another intersection in the tunnel. Further ahead was a faint glow of light emanating from above. A storm drain. It provided just enough light to see the widening stream of water and more graffiti on each of the walls.

Dennis turned to find Evan studying the cross section of the tunnel. He pulled a piece of paper and a pen out of his pocket and scribbled a couple lines to mark the section they had just traveled. He tried to remember how far each section was.

"I think this is it."

Dennis frowned. They were doing a lot of guessing. And now they were deep inside one of these tunnels. There was no way out quickly, which was never a good position to be in. Dennis suddenly whirled around when something clanged behind him. He instinctively drew his gun and laid it over his left wrist, flipping the flashlight around in his left hand.

The person caught in the beam of his flashlight abruptly stopped. It was a man dressed in dark clothes, dragging something behind him. His dark hair was long and matted and his wet beard glistened in the light.

Dennis stepped to his left, allowing him to peer past the man enough to see what he was dragging. It looked like a hockey stick. After a long pause, the man dropped his head from the glare and continued walking. He shuffled forward, passing between Dennis and Evan without a word.

After watching the man as he passed, Dennis then quietly slid his gun back into its holster.

Evan studied the paper again and looked up at him. He nodded his head, hesitantly in the direction the strange man had just come from.

"That way."

29

The Las Vegas flood tunnel project was originally planned for a staggering *one thousand* miles of underground channels. However, due to local budget cuts and competing projects, barely one-fifth of the project was ever completed and the abrupt ending left dozens of underground sections isolated and unfinished.

The finished tunnels worked well enough at redirecting water from most streets, so the remainder of the project was indefinitely postponed. And with the new problem for the Health and Human Services Department inside the tunnels, it only added to the mounting political and fiscal gridlock required to finish any more of the underground system. As a result, they were destined to remain in their current state for decades.

Seng turned into a small alley and killed his headlights. He slowed and rolled forward down the narrow, abandoned street. It was lined with trash and extended two blocks past a small group of old buildings, eventually terminating at a disintegrating concrete wall. At the base of the wall, more garbage stretched wide in both directions. It went beyond the asphalt and was piled shoulder-high. The area looked to be used as a dumping ground for the locally impoverished or, in some cases, those simply not interested in driving all the way to the dump.

Seng eased the Mercedes to a stop well away from

the largest heap. Keeping his lights off, he stepped out of the car and stood up. He raised his hand over his eyes to block the rain and scanned the area. A moment later, a dark figure emerged from behind one of the piles. He approached Seng in the increasing downpour and stopped at the hood of the car just as a second set of headlights turned into the alley, where it too turned off its lights.

The stolen Camry approached and quietly parked next to Seng's Mercedes. Inside, Kou turned off the engine and pushed the driver's door open, stepping carelessly into a puddle.

All three were Cambodian, and all three had grown up under the same brutal conditions. In Cambodia, they had seen people killed for petty reasons; in some cases, for no reason at all. As a result, life to them had a finite value. And it was an economic value much lower than most others could imagine.

The dark, expressionless faces of Seng and Kou nodded and followed their cohort, Bory. They approached the trash heap and circled around behind it nearer the wall. Bory reached down, pulling up an old mattress and then pushing it forward, to reveal a large circle in the middle of the unfinished street.

It was a manhole.

Katie jumped when she heard the familiar "clunk" above them. It was followed by the scraping of metal as the manhole cover was dragged open. Even with the darkness outside, some ambient light managed to fill the small section of tunnel below, allowing the three girls to see each other's outlines.

Katie looked up at the opening anxiously but froze

when she saw the familiar shape of Bory descend the metal rungs first. The second shape of Kou flooded her with fear, and she backed away from the others. *No!*

Yet it was when a small lamp was turned on that a surge of panic overtook her. They could clearly see the face of Seng climbing down behind the first two. It was the boss.

No! This wasn't right! It wasn't what she was expecting. Someone was coming to save them. She was sure. Her dream was real. It had to be. She stared in horror as Seng reached the bottom and peered around the dimly lit room.

He didn't come very often, but Katie could tell the look on his face was different this time. She didn't know what, but something was happening. She looked at Kou and Bory. They weren't carrying food or fresh supplies. Instead, Kou had something else in his hands: a knife and a giant roll of tape.

Deena looked up at the men with little more than curiosity, but Brooke turned to Katie with nervous eyes. This isn't what Katie had told her. She *said* help was coming!

Seng's voice was short and abrupt. "Come, we go up."

Deena stood quickly, and Brooke, already on her knees, rose slowly beside her. Brooke was still looking to Katie, who stared in stunned disbelief and shook her head. *No! No more!*

Seng watched the older girl back up. She knew something was coming. She continued backing up until she reached the makeshift barricade that cut them off from the rest of the tunnel. She wasn't going anywhere. Seng turned his attention back to the others and nodded at Kou, who then tore a piece of tape from the roll. It was just large enough to cover one of their mouths.

Bory took it and stepped forward, pressing the tape easily over Deena's mouth. He then grabbed Brooke's arm, yanking her toward him, and reached for another piece. Brooke turned and looked fearfully at Bory. *Katie had promised her.*

The tape went over Brooke's trembling lips and Bory's dirty, rough hand pressed it hard into place. The rest of the tape would be used when the girls were up the ladder and in the trunk of the Camry. Kou looked to Seng who nodded and gave them the "go ahead."

Katie watched as Deena and Brooke were pushed forward toward the ladder. She turned back to Seng, who was no longer watching the other girls. Instead, his eyes were fixed intently on her. It was at that moment that Katie made her decision. Much like her father, she wouldn't give up. What Seng didn't know was that during her time trapped in the darkness, Katie had probed the barricade behind her, which was nailed together with wood and pieces of old furniture. She had poked around and found a way around it. Until now, the moans and screams echoing down the damp tunnels were enough to keep her there, hoping that it would all end soon. But now she realized that being rescued was simply wishful thinking.

All at once she whirled around and fell onto the floor. She felt for the small opening and immediately pressed her head down against the cold concrete, forcing her head through.

"No!" yelled Seng, with wide eyes. He ran for her as Katie managed to wriggle her shoulders through followed by her tiny waist. Seng reached her just in time to see the last of her legs and feet disappear.

Seng fell onto the floor. His thin, muscular body slid and smashed headlong into the barricade. His arm jutted through the small opening and managed to grasp one of her ankles.

From the darkness on the other side, Katie felt the vice around her foot and screamed, kicking hard against Seng's wrist with her opposite foot. "NO! NO!" She felt around behind her and found something long and hard. It felt like a piece of wood. She pulled it to her and jammed it into Seng's wrist, which was now pulling her back toward the small opening. "NO! LET GO!" She pulled the piece of wood back and jammed it into him harder. Then again.

Katie couldn't see him let go, but she felt the sudden release and fell backward into several inches of water. She turned over, splashing, and scrambled to her feet.

An enraged Seng began smashing his body against the other side of the barricade, trying to break his way through.

Without the slightest hesitation, Katie turned and ran full speed into the pitch blackness.

30

A wave of dread washed over Evan the moment the beam from his flashlight hit the concrete. Just a moment before, a change in the sounds echoing through the tunnel told him something was wrong. The realization of seeing the dull gray wall in front of them was heart stopping. It was a dead end.

They were lost.

He blinked his eyes and stared at the wall a long time. He could almost feel the disappointment from Mr. Mayer standing behind him. Evan desperately reexamined the paper in his pocket. *But it looked right.*

He made a three hundred and sixty-degree scan with his flashlight, seeing only the path backward. He looked back at the dead end. The concrete in front of him was as old as the walls. There was no way forward.

Evan finally looked back at Mayer, helplessly. "I...I thought it was..." His voice trailed off as his mind now raced in an effort to figure out where he went wrong.

Dennis remained silent, but the look on his face was clear. It had been almost two hours, slogging through water and trash and *people*, fighting against a growing case of claustrophobia, only to find themselves lost now. Ironically, the only thing distracting him from the claustrophobia was the horrific stench.

He fought to stay calm and looked at Evan.

"Christ. Are we even close?"

Evan swallowed hard. He didn't want to say what he was thinking. *I don't know.* He could only watch as Mr. Mayer shook his head in frustration and turned around.

That was when they heard it.

They both stopped and peered into the darkness, listening. Dennis held out a hand to be quiet and closed his eyes, waiting. The next sound was louder.

He spun around only long enough to signal Evan to follow. In an instant, Dennis was running through the ankle-high water at full speed with his light bouncing up and down in front of him. The sound they had heard was a girl's screams.

And they were close.

31

Even through the splashing water, Katie could hear the barricade breaking apart in the darkness behind her. She screamed for help and kept running. Being unable to see anything in front of her was terrifying, so she kept one arm out in front as she ran, fearful of impacting something. But the terror behind her was a hundred times worse.

She knew Seng was now in the same tunnel and coming after her. How far away was he? The fear of having him grab her at any moment made Katie run even faster.

"HELP!"

Where were the people she'd heard before? They couldn't be that far away. Then she had a terrible thought. *What if she hadn't really heard screams after all? What if they were just strange noises that she mistook as human? What if there was no one else down here?* The sick realization hit her just before something large stopped her feet, sending her crashing forward into the water. She quickly raised her head and coughed.

Katie had no idea what she had tripped over and she didn't care. She struggled to get back on her feet, but it was too late. Seng had slowed when he heard the splash in front of him and managed only a partial trip in the darkness. He fell into Katie, knocking her small frame down again. But Seng managed to keep hold of her until he found her shoulders and wrapped a powerful right hand around her neck.

With his left, he reached up and wiped the water from his face. He adjusted his feet and brought both legs in tighter to keep her from thrashing. Raising his head to catch his breath, Seng then saw something further down the tunnel. He blinked and stared into the darkness.

Two small bright lights were dancing in the distance. Seng glanced down and grabbed the girl firmly with his second hand, looking back up. The lights were still there, bouncing back and forth. He stared at them for several seconds before noticing they were getting larger. His eyes suddenly grew wide.

Flashlights!

The lights that Seng saw were bouncing wildly now because Dennis Mayer was sprinting. He was running full speed and splashing heavily through the stream of water. A weakened Evan, struggling to keep up, had fallen back. He and Dennis could both see something now, farther down the tunnel. Two figures, one screaming for help. They were too far away to see their faces, but Evan knew who it was. It was Katie Keyes.

One of the lights was approaching faster than the other. Someone was coming quickly. Seng didn't know who it was, but he did know that trying to get the girl out of the tunnel in time was now impossible.

Yet he couldn't let her go. She was a witness and could identify him. She could identify all three of them.

He made a split second decision. Whoever was coming could have her. But she wouldn't be alive when they got there. With both hands, Seng forced the girl's face down into the water and kept it there.

Dennis' flashlight was now all but useless as he pumped his arms hard. The light was jumping uncontrollably and shining everywhere, except where he needed it. All he could see now was his own shadow, cast by Evan's flashlight behind him.

The screaming abruptly stopped, which only caused Mayer to run harder.

Seng kept the girl down, her face still below the water. He was thankful for her struggling. He had very little time now and it would make the end come faster.

What Seng didn't know, what he couldn't know, was that Dennis Mayer was *fast*. Having been a hurdler in high school, he could still outrun some of the department's new recruits, even in his forties. And now at full sprint, he was closing the distance quickly, praying that nothing was in his way.

The shock on Seng's face came within seconds as he realized just how quickly the silhouette was moving toward him. He could see the splashing of the water with every step and the outline of a large man barreling down. He immediately let go of the girl and stood up.

He was out of time. He had to get out. He turned to run and stumbled over the object which had tripped both him and the girl. It was too late. The large figure was now practically on him, and with a final leap forward, he sailed over the girl and hit Seng like a locomotive. In one violent collision, they both crashed to the ground.

Behind him, Evan reached Katie where she kneeled, coughing and trying to regain her breath. Her wet hair was plastered to her face, and she shielded her eyes from Evan's flashlight. Her condition left her almost unrecognizable from the pictures he'd seen, but he knew it was her.

In front of them, Dennis rolled onto a knee and stood up to face Seng, who was already on his feet. Despite his flashlight being on the ground and half submerged, he could still see Seng's hand disappear behind him and reemerge with a long knife.

Dennis quickly reached for his gun and found an empty holster. He stepped back, searching the ground for it. Nothing. He quickly backed away and frantically searched again. There was nothing but water at his feet. He looked back up at the eerily shadowed face of Seng and the gleaming knife in his hand. The Cambodian's mouth spread into a wicked grin.

"Evan!" Dennis called over his shoulder. "Get her out of here!"

With some effort, Evan pulled Katie up to her feet and looked back into the dark void from which they'd come. He wasn't sure he could find the way back out, and even if he could, the water was rising rapidly with the hundreds of streets funneling rainwater into the tunnels.

Dennis knew what Evan was thinking and without looking back, answered his question. "This way!" he exclaimed, pointing past Seng.

All at once, Dennis sprang forward, closing the distance between him and Seng. He saw the glint of the knife flash just before both men collided. With a grunt, Dennis grabbed Seng's arms and threw his weight forward, smashing him against one of the concrete walls.

Evan was already moving. He ran past them pulling Katie, who was stumbling behind him.

They ran quickly in spite of Katie's attempts to clear the wet hair from her eyes. She struggled to see the ground as they splashed forward through the running water, eventually tripping only to have Evan pull her back to her feet.

It wasn't until Evan wriggled through and pulled Katie past that she looked back and recognized the broken barricade. She immediately panicked and dug her feet in, trying to stop. "No! NO!"

Evan searched the makeshift room and spotted the open hole above. Rungs ran up the wall to the surface. "Come on!" he cried. "Hurry!"

"No!" Katie resisted and dug in harder, crying desperately. "There's more! There's more!"

Already halfway across the room, Evan stopped and looked at her. "More what?"

"More of *them!*" She pointed to the opening above them. "Up there!"

He allowed Katie to pull him back a few steps as he hesitated and peered upward. "There's more? Are you sure?"

"Yes!"

"How many?"

"Two. They already took Deena and Brooke. If they see us, they're going to get us too!"

Evan's eyes grew nervous. They were trapped. They couldn't get out. They would never make it past Mr. Mayer and the other man again, and even if they could, they might drown trying to find their way back through the tunnels. But now their only alternative was to climb up where two more men were waiting for them. To make matters worse, Evan was still weak and doubted he could fight one, let alone two.

He tried to think as Katie continued trying to pull him backward. Maybe he could fight long enough for her to escape. But then what? They would just finish him off and then get her again.

He turned back and shined his light on the barricade. What about Mr. Mayer? Was he okay? If he was, then he could help. But if he wasn't...Seng could be coming for them.

Evan wearily abandoned the manhole and faced the barricade. He had a better chance of fighting one man than two. Even if it was only long enough to allow Katie to make a run for it. It was the best chance they had.

At that moment, a frightening realization washed over him. He was not going to make it out of there. He was probably going to die tonight in those tunnels.

He heard the sound of splashing footsteps approaching from beyond the barricade. Someone was coming.

He handed his flashlight to Katie and rushed forward, wrenching a piece of board free from the barricade.

"Can you run?" he asked, in a low voice.

"Yes."

He nodded and took a deep breath, gripping the board tight with both hands. This was it.

"EVAN!"

He quickly glanced around and looked expectantly at Katie's face, staring up at him from the darkness. It took only a moment to realize she hadn't said anything. After that, it took only a split second longer for Evan to place the voice that called his name.

A voice that was impossible.

32

He heard it again and looked up at the manhole's dark ring.

"Evan! Where are you?"

As the voice grew nearer, a burst of light found the manhole and suddenly shone down through the opening, searching. Evan yanked Katie back around and ran to the light. With squinting eyes, he peered up through the large hole to see a silhouette behind another flashlight.

"Tania?"

"Evan!" Her eyes opened wide with excitement. "Thank God!"

"Wha…" Evan began to speak but stopped at the sound of the splashes in the tunnel growing nearer.

"Climb up, Evan!"

He took a step forward but felt Katie's grip stop him again. He paused and peered up with one eye closed. "Is it safe?"

Neither could see the smile on Tania's face. "Yeah, you could say that."

He quickly grabbed Katie and lifted her up to the first rung on the wall. "Don't worry," he whispered. "She's with me."

Without another word, Katie gripped the rungs and climbed up toward the light. Evan followed closely behind her.

He reached the top as Katie was lifted out of the hole. He popped his head out and looked around.

Piles of what appeared to be garbage surrounded them. "What are you doing here?" he cried. Tania grabbed his free hand and pulled him out. "And how did you know where to find us?"

Tania motioned past the garbage. Curiously, Evan peered over one of the piles. He could see the top of a car roof, but when he stepped closer, he almost couldn't believe his eyes.

Two cars were parked side by side, sitting silently in the dark. One looked old, and the other new and expensive. But it was what he saw on the ground that really surprised him. A man's figure was lying alongside one of the cars. Further back, the legs of the second figure were protruding out from behind the car's back bumper.

In front, sitting quietly on the ground and leaning against the car's grill, was the last person Evan expected to see.

He looked half dead, his arms resting on the ground on either side, trying to keep himself up. In his right hand, Dan Taylor held what looked to be a tire iron.

Taking Katie's hand again, Evan began to approach but stopped at the sound of someone climbing the rungs below.

Evan glanced worriedly at Tania. He steered Katie toward her and desperately looked for a new weapon. A dark head emerged from out of the large hole, searching for them. Upon spotting them, the figure raised the large knife, covered in something dark, and prepared to climb out.

"Run!" Evan shouted, backing up.

The figure watched them for a long moment before shaking his head. "Well, I'm sure as hell not gonna chase you."

Evan gasped. He ran forward until he could see Mayer's face. "You're alive!"

"I hope so," he groaned. Dennis slowly reached his arms out of the hole and practically pulled himself out. With a wince, he rolled onto the ground and stared at Katie. "Please tell me you're Katie."

"Yes."

"Thank God," he said, and rolled onto his back. "Now get me to a hospital."

Evan spotted blood coming from Dennis' shirt and quickly took off his own jacket. He balled it up and pressed it hard into Dennis' side. Clutching it with his own hand, Dennis peered up into the night sky and tried to slow his breathing. After a minute, he turned his head and looked at Tania.

"How the hell did you get here?"

She grinned and looked back to the cars where Taylor was still sitting on the ground, exhausted. "He made me drive him."

With some effort, Dennis managed to stand up enough to see Taylor. "I'll be damned."

"What about Deena and Brooke?" Katie asked Tania.

"They're hiding in one of the cars. We didn't know who else was down there." She turned to Evan. "But Mr. Taylor was sure *you* were here."

33

Anne Keyes lifted her head off the sofa at the sound of the doorbell. After clearing her head and noticing what little sunlight there was outside, she checked her watch. It was 7:30 a.m.

The doorbell rang again.

Keyes blinked and slowly stood up. Who would be at her door this early? There was no search today. As she walked forward, she glanced back at the couch and recalled the previous evening. The depression was taking its toll.

She reached the front door and unlocked the deadbolt. When she pulled it open, she was surprised to see a woman standing alone on her porch.

"Ms. Keyes?"

"Yes."

"I'm from Social Services. I wanted to come by and introduce myself and ask you a few questions.

Keyes sighed. *More questions.* "Isn't it a little early?"

"It is. I'm sorry about that. I was in the area and was hoping it wouldn't be a problem. I know you've held several early morning searches and wasn't sure if you were coordinating another today."

"No. Not today." Keyes shook her head and pushed the screen door open. "Come in."

The woman pulled the screen door the rest of the way open and stepped inside. She quietly closed both the screen and front door behind her. She then watched a tired Anne Keyes return and sit back down onto her couch.

The living room was very nice. Clean and well decorated. Many women in emotional distress fell back to cleaning their house, almost as a form of mindless therapy. Something that allowed them to remain productive, keeping their minds on something else. Anything else.

The woman approached the couch, examining some pictures on the wall. "Is this your husband?"

"Yes," Keyes replied, wearily. "He died two years ago."

"I'm sorry." The woman took a seat across from her. "Ms. Keyes, I know this has been a terrible time for you, but during an ongoing investigation, we like to check in on the family. To provide emotional or any other kind of support we can. It's not uncommon for family and friends to suffer from various forms of emotional trauma, so we try to look out for any symptoms. Things that might allow us to avoid looming problems."

Keyes almost laughed. "*Now* you want to check on the family? I'd say you're a little late. You might try helping the families when the trauma actually occurs. Before they lose months of sleep. Or before they can't eat for weeks at a time." Keyes' eyes became solemn. "Before they've lost hope," she added under her breath.

The woman frowned and gently adjusted her rectangular glasses. "I'm sorry. I know the timing is not ideal. Unfortunately, the county is pretty understaffed."

Keyes stared at her for a moment, and then looked away with a shrug.

"Are you on any medication, Ms. Keyes?"

She almost scoffed. "No. I'm not on any medication. I probably should be."

"Have you been experiencing any symptoms like sweating, dizziness? Maybe trembling or shaking hands?"

"No."

"Upset stomach?"

"No." Keyes stopped as if just realizing what she was saying. She examined the woman in front of her curiously. "What was your name?"

"My name is Shannon. Shannon Mayer."

Anne Keyes didn't know that the woman in front of her wasn't sent by Social Services. And she wasn't there as part of her daughter's investigation. Instead, she was there to try to assess Keyes' current mental and emotional state. To gauge whether, after what she had been through, Keyes was prepared for another emotional shock.

Shannon understood better than almost anyone the strain which Anne Keyes had been through. She also understood that while some people possessed a certain innate emotional resilience, others did not. And what Anne Keyes was about to experience could be as traumatic as anything experienced so far.

It took several seconds for Shannon's last name to sink in for Keyes. Shannon watched the recognition form in the woman's eyes.

"Mayer?" she asked questioningly.

"That's right."

Keyes stared at her, thinking. Was the name a coincidence? If so, she had sworn secrecy to the man and had to be careful. She cleared her throat and chose her words deliberately. "Do you know anyone named Dennis?"

Shannon smiled. "He's my husband."

"Your husband?!"

Shannon nodded and stood up, before calmly crossing the living room. She returned to the front door and flipped on the switch for the outside light.

The woman's gaze followed Shannon with a puzzled expression. Anne Keyes returned to the other side of the room and remained standing.

"And you're with Social Services?"

The corner of Shannon's lip curled. "Actually, I'm not. I'm sorry I lied to you." She watched Keyes grow increasingly confused.

"I don't understand."

"Ms. Keyes, I'm not with the county. But I *am* here to assess you. I'm a psychiatrist."

"Assess me. Assess me for what?"

"For this."

Shannon turned and glanced out the front window as a small car stopped at the curb. Keyes turned and followed Shannon's eyes through the wide pane of glass just as two of the car doors opened: one on the driver's side and the other on the rear passenger side nearest to her.

"What's going…?" She stopped midsentence when she recognized the driver of the car: the teenager she'd met just a few days before. Her eyes darted to the passenger door where an attractive teenage girl stepped out. But it was when the third person got out of the car that Anne Keyes suddenly gasped and brought both hands to her mouth.

The young girl stepped out of the car, dressed in new clothes. She looked briefly at the house before spotting her mother through the front window.

Inside, her mother gripped Shannon's arm, the counselor having quietly stepped closer to her. "OH, MY GOD!"

Shannon sensed Anne's knees begin to buckle and quickly wrapped an arm around her waist. "Deep breaths."

On the front lawn, Katie took a tentative step forward before bursting into a run as fast as her legs could carry her.

"KATIE!" her mother screamed. "KATIE!" She stumbled toward the door with Shannon still at her side. She only made it halfway when her daughter threw the door open.

Katie immediately darted across the room, directly into her mother's open, trembling arms.

Anne collapsed onto her knees with Katie still tight against her and began sobbing uncontrollably. "My baby! My baby!"

Twelve-year-old Katie never looked up. She simply pressed her head into her mother's chest and cried. At that moment, no one else in the world existed.

No one.

34

It took a long time for them to finally separate. When they did, Anne wiped her eyes with her hands and looked around the room, finding Shannon at the front door, smiling. Evan and Tania stood behind her on the doorstep.

"I…I don't know what to say. I…"

"You don't need to say anything," Shannon said. "Just remember our deal."

She spoke to Evan, who was smiling at her and her daughter. "Not a word."

Shannon watched her silently lay a cheek back down onto the top of Katie's head before stepping out and closing the door behind her.

Of course, Anne Keyes would *have* to say something. The Bakersfield police would arrive soon, along with a swarm of reporters. But before that, she would receive a phone call explaining exactly what to say and what not to say. It wasn't foolproof, but it was the best they could manage.

As for Katie, it would be a long time before she realized that the word "heaven" sounded almost exactly like *Evan*.

On her way home, Shannon would also make an anonymous call to one of Bakersfield's local support organizations. Anne and her daughter were going to need a lot of counseling. Their recovery was just beginning.

She thought about Dan Taylor. It was true that helping was fraught with danger. Putting yourself out there meant there was only so much you could control. She wondered what would happen if Taylor could witness the experience of delivering a child home safely. Would he then accept that perhaps the risk was worth it?

Later that day, the extra-wide door opened inward, and Shannon stepped into the hospital room. She glanced briefly at the single chair and white cabinet when she came around the corner. She found Dennis asleep in his bed. An IV was attached to his left arm and bruises covered his face.

His eyes opened as she approached.

"I'm sorry, were you sleeping?"

He shook his head, gently. "Nah."

Shannon sat down on the edge of his bed and picked up his free hand, wrapping her hands around his. "How are you feeling?"

"Pretty good, actually." Dennis pressed a large blue button on the bed, raising himself up. "I'll be out tomorrow."

"Good."

Dennis pulled his hand away and gently brushed a strand of brown hair out of Shannon's face. "You sure are beautiful."

She smiled and leaned down to kiss him. When she came back up, Dennis took a deep breath and pushed himself up in the bed.

"How did the delivery go?"

"Good. Really good, actually."

"They're both okay?"

"Yes. Her mother wasn't showing any serious anxiety or dislocation symptoms, and Katie was already coming around by the time we arrived. The next couple months will be hard, but with treatment, they should come out okay."

Of course, Shannon knew that "okay" was a relative statement. Intense emotional trauma was, by its very nature, unpredictable. But the two Keyes both displayed signs of natural resilience, which made all the difference. Many were not as fortunate. Deena, one of the other girls, and her parents had a much harder road ahead of them.

"And how's Evan?"

"Good. He seems to be embracing things pretty well." Shannon stopped and grinned at the thought. "Perhaps even literally at the moment."

Dennis laughed and clutched his side, moaning. "They're a good match, aren't they?"

"They sure are."

He breathed easy and grabbed Shannon's hand again. With a roll of his head, he looked out the room's window at the thick gray clouds and the giant Las Vegas city sprawl below it. "At least I have a room with a view."

She winked. "I'm sure it's an extra cost."

He smiled but kept staring out. "And what about Taylor?"

"He's gone."

Dennis turned back to her.

"After a long talk with Evan, he left on foot. Headed home. He said he's not ready for a life of searching for lost children."

Dennis frowned. "Not *ready*, huh?"

"I think he has other issues to work through.

There's clearly a lot in his past he hasn't told us."

"Not that he ever would have."

"That's probably true." Shannon sighed and changed the subject. "So, have the police talked to you?"

"They were here this morning for almost two hours."

"And?"

Dennis shrugged. "I explained that I had tracked down those Cambodians on the street. They already had a reputation, so it wasn't all that unbelievable. I said I followed them into that alley and waited for them with the tire iron."

"And they believed you?"

"Not really. There are some inconsistencies, but they're much more interested in digging deeper to find who else those three guys were working with rather than how they met their maker. And trust me, the thought of these thugs standing before their maker is going to bring them a smile for a long time."

"What about the girls?"

"The detective will want to talk to them at some point but probably more as a formality. They just want to see the kids home safe, like anyone else."

"I'm sure." She reached down, straightening his gown, looking at him with love in her eyes. He really was an amazing man. Neither of them would ever take things for granted again.

"So, is Evan going to hang things up?"

Shannon smirked and stood up. "I don't think so."

"What do you mean?"

She answered amusedly as she walked back toward the door. "I mean I'm pretty sure he's just waiting for you to get out of here."

Dennis began to speak but stopped when Shannon disappeared back around the corner. His heart quickened when he heard her open the door.

A few moments later, she returned with Ellie who stood nervously at her side. Her young eyes grew wide with concern when she saw the bruises on his face.

They both stared at each other until he smiled and spread his arms. "Hey, Pumpkin."

Ellie wiped her tears away and ran to her father. "I was worried about you, Daddy."

Dennis Mayer lowered his good arm to scoop her up onto the bed and felt her tiny arms wrap around his neck and squeeze. His eyes filled with tears.

35

The light drizzle continued for a third day, preventing anything from drying out. The air was warm, but the damp leaves covering the ground acted as a thin, slippery blanket, making traction difficult. The area had some of the densest foliage in the Malibu Creek State Park, making it a better hiding spot than most, particularly for things that took time to hide.

Evan stood quietly on a small hillside, trying to keep his footing in spite of the slick leaves. Another shiver ran through him as he leaned into the slope, trying to detect the voices far above him. His waiting had nothing to do with being able to climb the hill. He'd already done that.

Evan knew what they were going to find. And he didn't want to be there to see it. He couldn't. It was too difficult. He wanted to make sure they were found, but he couldn't watch it happen. Instead, he waited out of sight while they dug.

He finally heard the sound of wet, squishing footsteps headed toward him. Several seconds later he saw a figure appear above and slowly make his way down the embankment. He was a Lieutenant with the Los Angeles Police Department and a friend of Dennis Mayer. A man that Mr. Mayer said could be trusted. Along with a few discreet others, these officers all made sure the rest were found.

Black, the man who shot at them in Bakersfield,

turned out to have a lot more to hide than they could have imagined. The secret room in his house implicated both him and his brother in several kidnappings. And Dan Taylor was right. Walking into that hidden room made him sicker than he could imagine. But he had to find them.

And they did find them. All eight. But they were far too late. Evan deeply wished they had found out sooner. The sense of loss he felt left him almost as sick as being in that terrible room.

Though with the help of Mr. Mayer's friends, they found them and took them home. These deliveries he couldn't watch, but knowing they were with their families again still gave him some comfort.

The solemn look in the Lieutenant's eyes let Evan know that they'd found the last one. He nodded and turned around to descend the hill. When he reached the bottom, Evan walked out onto the small pasture's bright green grass. He closed his eyes and tilted his head back, feeling the light drops of the rain on his face.

He knew there were more out there. More he could still save. And he was going to save as many as he could.

AFTERWORD

There was something indescribable about the beauty of the Pacific Northwest. The dark green pine trees layered against the gray and white background of the Sierra Nevada Mountains were truly something to behold. Topped with a crystal blue sky, it felt like viewing a window into heaven.

Dan Taylor leaned forward in his seat, gazing into "God's country," with his breath just close enough to fog a small corner of the window. The train curved to the right, allowing him to glimpse the distant train tracks as they wound in and around the snow-covered passes.

Without a word, he stared at the fog as it seemed to crawl across the glass before disappearing just as quickly. It was the only indication of the frigid temperature outside.

The seat next to Taylor was empty, which was fortunate. His large frame would have made a tight fit. Instead he relaxed, twisting slightly in his seat and watching the scene pass by in amazing grandeur.

Evan should have been able to locate the other children by now. Hopefully, he stayed away during the exhuming. Connections with the dead were very powerful, like a magnet, whether you were in the fog or not. It made coming back *from out of the fog* more difficult. In many ways, death was like a black hole. Much more powerful than it looked and once too close, there was no return.

Taylor couldn't deny his feeling of remorse over leaving the kid. An emotion he hadn't felt in a very long time. Evan was bright and exceptionally gifted. And there was something about him that made Evan immediately likable, something Taylor wondered if he was even aware of. More than all of that, the kid had a longing to help. A need so deeply inborn that he didn't think Evan would ever stop. He would continue sacrificing himself for others until one day it went too far. One day it would get too close and the fog would take him.

Taylor had initially seen it as foolishness. Recklessness, really. But now he wasn't so sure. Now, he viewed things differently. He realized how truly empty a life of hiding had left him. Decades that could have been used for something meaningful. Instead of hiding, he could have been helping someone. Like those children. Even if not right away, he could have eventually done something.

Yet his fear had won out. Fear that they would find him again. And this time they wouldn't make the same mistakes. They would dissect him like a lab rat to understand how he worked.

Taylor sat quietly, swaying with the side to side motion of the train. As the tracks rounded again, a giant mountain came into view. Timeless, the peak towered above, its granite cliffs spotted with white patches of snow. He gazed up as they passed. It was ageless. Frozen in time and completely unaware of the tiny speck of machinery passing beneath it. Unaware and uncaring.

Taylor wondered how long it had been there. Millions of years, at least. He wondered how many specks had lived and died before that very mountain.

As Taylor stared upward, he was overcome by his own mortality. No, it was more than that. It was a feeling of utter insignificance. Insignificance of a life that was nothing more than a tiny blip along an incomprehensible timeline. The briefest of flashes. One so fast and so small and virtually unnoticeable. How many billions of things lived and died in that same blip of time without ever making a *ripple* in the world around them? It was as if the earth had never known they existed.

He thought about fate. Would his life be the same? Nothing more than a flash in time, and then disappear without a trace? Without anyone knowing he was ever there. What was the point? What was the point of living if it meant leaving no impact or *ripple* at all?

It was worse than that. Dan Taylor was unique. Unique in a way that virtually no one else was. Whether it was a curse or a gift didn't matter. It was an ability that few had ever heard of, and only a handful had probably experienced. And what did he choose to do? Hide away and live a life of nothingness.

Hiding out of fear. *Fear of what...pain? Fear of death?* Everything died. Everything. Including him. How many of those billions of life forms died in permanent obscurity?

Taylor leaned back in his chair. He stared at the floor, blinking. It wasn't about how you died. *It was about how you lived.*

And he wasn't living at all.

He thought about those bastards. The spooks at the CIA. They'd driven him underground. They'd driven him into a life of fear and nothingness.

He shook his head. *Christ, were they even looking for him anymore? Any of them?*

It had been over twenty years. Technology was leaps and bounds beyond what it was then. Today governments could spy with impunity, and they did. Every time you touched something with a computer chip, it left a trail. Now they could see everything and they could do anything. To anyone.

What he did for the government then was now done by a fleet of satellites and drones. *What could they possibly want with him anymore? Nothing, that's what. He was still hiding...from something that happened two decades ago.*

Taylor frowned. Good or bad, he had an ability that could allow him to leave a ripple. How many people could make their brief flash in the universe actually mean something?

It wasn't about him anymore. And it had taken a damn teenager to show him.

Despite the freezing temperature outside, the home kept most rooms at a comfortable seventy-five degrees since many of their tenants had trouble staying warm. And they *were* considered "tenants," until they moved into a full-time care facility inside, which they were then deemed "patients."

For now, at eighty-three, Margaret was still years away from being a "patient." But it was days like this that made her wonder. Today something didn't feel right. She remained in her chair, inside her small room, staring outside at the falling snow. It was quiet. Only the ticking of the small clock on her dresser disturbed the stillness.

Margaret let her head fall forward slightly, trying to determine how serious her symptoms were. There was no pain, but she was just so tired. Her arms and legs felt unusually heavy. Her eyes moved to the small table nearby where a small electronic "bell" rested next to one of her magazines.

She heard the soft squeaking of footsteps behind her. "Margaret?" The voice was from her nurse, Elaine. Thank God.

A moment later, Elaine appeared at her side and studied her. "How are you feeling?"

Margaret blinked her tired eyes and struggled to raise her head. It was hard to form words. "Tired."

"Are you in any pain?"

She thought about the question and answered slowly. "No pain."

Her nurse patted her arm gently. "Good."

Margaret didn't know that the medication Elaine had given her just fifteen minutes earlier contained something more than her normal prescription: a drug that was causing her current condition.

"I'll be right back, Margaret." Her nurse straightened and abruptly disappeared from view before she could respond.

"Wait," was all Margaret could manage. But Elaine was gone.

The nurse closed the door behind her and looked down the hall. When the door clicked shut, she walked toward the two people standing nearby. "Okay. She's ready."

"Are you sure?"

"Yes."

Elaine looked at her supervisor who then turned to the man standing next her. Silently, the man followed Elaine back to the door where she placed a hand on the knob. She looked up at him with raised eyebrows.

Together they opened the door and stepped inside. She crossed the small room and stood in front of the elderly woman, this time feeling for her pulse. "How do you feel, Margaret?"

Margaret didn't answer. She merely stared at her nurse with glazed eyes.

Elaine looked up and over the old woman's head, giving a nod to the man behind her.

Given both her health and her age, this was the only way to be safe. Very slowly, he stepped forward and stood behind the nurse, who was still examining Margaret. When he was seated behind her, Elaine slowly stepped aside and out of the way, allowing the old woman to see the man sitting in front of her.

The recognition was immediate. Even in her dazed state, she gasped and opened her eyes wide as if seeing a ghost.

It had been so very long. Dan Taylor leaned forward in his chair and smiled tenderly. He reached forward and placed his hand on top of hers.

"Hi, Mom. It's me, Danny."

The late afternoon sun was dropping quickly now, nearly gone behind the shadow of the Appalachians far in the distance. Headlights were already lighting up Dulles Road as thousands of commuters on their way home snaked past the large but infamous building. Located on Sunset Hills Road, the two giant buildings were easily visible to anyone traveling along Virginia's State Route 267, especially in slow traffic.

Surprisingly unassuming in appearance, they were as controversial, if not more so, than the White House located less than twenty miles away. However, while the White House was the center of media attention and thousands, if not millions, of photographs, the main offices of the Central Intelligence Agency went to great efforts to minimize their "visual footprint" by eliminating nearly all pictures of its location from various digital maps and databases. And everyone knew why.

The CIA's reputation was world-renowned. The agency had been involved in some of the darkest moments in U.S. history. It was the very definition of clandestine and had tentacles spread much further around the globe than even the public suspected. In fact, most high-level operatives joked that if the public ever learned of the truth behind the doors of the CIA, it would cause a revolution overnight.

Of course, there was no way to know if that were true. And to many, it was an insignificant concern. The might of the U.S. government was too powerful to be scaled back now. Their skills at propaganda and diversion through public scandals had long been honed to a science. It no longer mattered who was in

181

office. When too much truth was revealed, intentionally or accidentally, the release of compromising information, followed by an arrest and multiple leaks to the press, was enough to distract most of the public until the excitement passed. And those who cared and were actually paying attention controlled too few votes to matter.

Public perception was a science now, fine-tuned and perfected through the last fifty years of modern media channels. And the CIA was the most masterful of all government departments.

Yet even among the unhallowed halls, the night was usually quiet. Mild snowfall and the upcoming Christmas holiday left most of the building's offices vacant, except just a few with their lights still on.

In one such office, a man sat quietly behind a large elaborate desk, typing on his keyboard. With hair that was neat and gray, he glanced up at his screen through dark-framed glasses. His face was worn but strong.

He looked up at his office door when it suddenly opened inward.

"You're still here. Good."

Without the slightest change in expression, the man behind the desk moved his hands away from the keyboard and straightened.

"I was asked to stop by and give you this." While crossing the room, the visitor reached inside his jacket and retrieved a large envelope. He laid it down when he reached the desk.

Director Douglass Bollinger stared at the envelope before finally stretching forward to pick it up. "What is it?"

"Pictures. From our new NGI system."

The FBI's New Generation Identification system had been revealed to the public in the fall of 2014. It was an advanced facial recognition system designed to house over fifty million faces in a massive database. It was sold to the public as a tool in the war on terror, but most government departments knew it was designed for something far grander. Fifty million images were merely the beginning.

"We've now begun rolling the system out into some other metropolitan hubs, beginning with larger train and bus stations. These images were picked up in Los Angeles a few days ago. The system flagged them, and Mr. Brennan asked that I deliver these to you personally. As a Christmas present."

"Is that right?" Bollinger was rhetorical. He slid the large 8 ½ x 11 pictures out and examined them.

There were several faces in the picture and it took Bollinger a moment to see him. When he did, his expression froze.

After a long silence, he finally blinked and moved on to the next picture. Each time he saw the face, his heart began to beat faster.

"Mr. Brennan said you would know who he was."

Bollinger didn't hear him. He was stuck, staring again at the last picture. *Impossible.*

"I take it you know him." Still no answer. Finally, he shrugged and turned. "I guess I'll show myself out."

Bollinger didn't notice the young agent leave. Nor did he hear the sound of the door clicking shut behind him. Instead, the large office fell silent with the only sound being the racing of Bollinger's heart.

He couldn't believe it. Dan Taylor was alive.

ABOUT THE AUTHOR

Michael Grumley lives in Northern California with his wife and two young daughters. His email address is michael@michaelgrumley.com, and his web site is www.michaelgrumley.com where you can find supplemental Q&A pages for his books, as well as a very unique offer.

MESSAGE FROM THE AUTHOR

Thank you for taking the time to read *The Unexpected Hero*. I hope you enjoyed the second installment of Evan's story. As some of you may know, I'm a part-time, self-published author, with the goal of being able to write full-time. Not surprisingly, a self-published writer's only real means for accomplishing this is through reviews and referrals. I know leaving a review can be a bit of a pain, but if you could please spare two minutes to leave a review for The Unexpected Hero, I would be very grateful.

Michael

Click her to leave a review for The Unexpected Hero.

OTHER BOOKS BY
MICHAEL GRUMLEY

BREAKTHROUGH

LEAP

AMID THE SHADOWS

THROUGH THE FOG

THE UNEXPECTED HERO

Made in the USA
San Bernardino, CA
28 May 2020